The Three Candles Of Little Veronica

The story of a child's soul
in this world and the other

by Manfred Kyber

*Translated from the German
by Rosamond Reinhardt*

*Illustrations by Iris Guarducci
Decorations by Doris Karsell*

NEW EDITION

WALDORF PRESS, PUBLISHERS
Adelphi University
Garden City, New York 11530

AVAILABLE IN ENGLISH BY THE SAME AUTHOR

Among Animals, Centaur Press Limited, London, 1967

This edition was made with the kind permission of
Mrs. Leonie Alt-Kyber
Hesse & Becker Verlag, Rottach-Egern, Germany

Translation copyright © 1972 by Rosamond Reinhardt
Copyright © 1972 by The Waldorf Institute
   for Liberal Education, Garden City, New York
Copyright © 1975 by Waldorf Press, Publishers,
   Garden City, New York

Library of Congress card number 75-1960

ISBN 0-914614-05-3

Printed in the Unites States of America for the Waldorf Press by The Studley Press, Inc.

DEDICATION

Franz E. Winkler, M.D. [1907 - 1972] loved the story of Little Veronica, encouraged its translation, and by his own life gave substance to the ideals for which it speaks. The editors of the Waldorf Press wish to express their gratitude to him for setting in motion the circumstances that have made this remarkable story available to the English-speaking world.

Contents

Introduction

Even a short time before the age of motor traffic, the lonely northern countryside along the Baltic coast of Germany was considerably more deserted than it is today. In that age and physical setting Manfred Kyber chose to place his story.

Human dwellings were few and far between. Castle Irreloh stood alone and sinister, listening to the eternal song of the sea. Some said it was haunted, but no one knew, for their eyes had become accustomed to this world alone. From Irreloh it was several miles to the little town of Halmar: Halmar, with its narrow winding streets and old houses dominated by the church spire; Halmar, with its sturdy townsmen, its worthy Pastor Haller; Halmar, with the ghosts that walked its narrow streets unguessed at.

A fortunate few carry with them through life the vision of the innocent years. The rest of us must work hard to retrieve the light that is so freely given to us at birth. But if, in reverence for all life, in patient observation, in sorrow and in compassion, the veil of darkness falls from our eyes, then it is we who are the lucky ones. For in full consciousness we have reached back into Paradise before the Fall. We have earned that which every child inherits unearned.

So, if we are to make sense of the story of Halmar, of Irreloh, of Pastor Haller, of Ulla Uhlberg, of Peter, of Johannes Wanderer, and, above all, of Little Veronica herself, we must look at their world with the unclouded eyes of a child. Such eyes will not give us a fairy-tale picture of life. Rather will they reveal the living truth that lies hidden in all fairy tales.

R.R.

The translator is deeply grateful to her husband, George Reinhardt, for his patient help. A real-life Master Mützchen, he guided her around the steepest thresholds and steps which, as in the House of Shadows, lurk within the German language. Such help was invaluable in the attempt to interpret as accurately as possible the subtle thought of Manfred Kyber.

Who with the eye of reverence may discern
How crystals form within the soul of Earth,
Watch in the quickening seed the clear flame burn,
In life see death, and in decay new birth . . .
He who has found his kin in man and beast
And in that kinship God's own Brotherhood,
At the High Table of the Grail shall feast,
Sup with the Lord of Love, taste holy food . . .
He, seeking, finds (God's promise shall suffice)
The pathway to forgotten Paradise.

Manfred Kyber

CHAPTER I

IN THE GARDEN OF SPIRITS

ITTLE Veronica sat playing in the sand in a Garden of Spirits. But you must not think this was some special garden, because it was not special at all. As well as a great many trees, all sorts of other things grew there: potatoes, cabbages, and radishes were set out beside one another in long, neat, orderly rows, while roses and lilies shone red and white in the early summer sunshine.

It was a large garden, completely enclosed by a high wall, crumbling and moss-covered: a quiet, withdrawn world, as all old gardens are. At one end, hidden behind flowering shrubs, was a little baroque garden-house where Uncle Johannes lived, and at the other end stood a great gray building, some hundreds of years old, and this was Little Veronica's home. It was called the House of Shadows. But I can only explain about this later on, because at this time Little Veronica did not really know she was living in it at all. She was still living completely in the Garden of Spirits; and though it seemed like an ordinary enough garden, Little Veronica, as I told you, saw it with her inner eyes—the eyes she had brought with her from heaven—and for such eyes as these every garden is a Garden of Spirits, and the whole world is an ocean of life and light. We all once saw the Earth in this way when we were children, but then came the great twilight, our clear vision was dimmed, and now we have forgotten everything. But I want to bring back to you what you have forgotten, as I myself remember it out of the darkness and the twilight.

Look deep into life and into the light, Little Veronica, before the eyes of heaven fall asleep. Then you will have something to remember when the twilight comes and darkness is all about you. It grows dark around everyone so that each may painfully become aware and thus find himself in the darkness—himself and God. But it is a long road. It is hard for us that we must all walk it.

Little Veronica's spade and her pail with its gaily painted red bunny lay idle by a newly dug flowerbed where she meant to plant some extra special things. But now she was sitting still, gazing wide-eyed and astonished at the garden. To her eyes which were still the eyes of heaven, the quite ordinary garden was a Garden of Spirits. How much there was here to see and to hear!

"Wouldn't you like to see my country-house, Veronica?" asked a big beetle who was sitting in front of her, as he saluted her with his feeler.

"See how white our blossoms are," said the spirits of the Lilies. "So pure and so white is the heavenly garment you once wore."

"Have you noticed how cleverly my children can roll themselves together?" asked the Hedgehog mother, who was sitting with her family in a comfortable hole in the moss-covered wall.

"Look how red our cups are," said the Rose-souls. "So pure and so red is the chalice of the Grail, to which you once stretched out your arms. You don't think about it any more now, but you will remember it, Little Veronica, when the twilight has come down upon you."

"Don't you think my children fly beautifully?" asked the Blackbird, with a challenging thrust of her beak. "How exactly they land again on the edge of the nest! And what's more, they haven't practiced it very long, but no one would guess it. Such skill! Have you ever seen anything like it?"

The cabbage leaves rustled, while butterflies flitted overhead.

"You are like us, Little Veronica; you are a caterpillar, and later you'll turn into a butterfly. You will become a chrysalis when the twilight comes."

The radishes nudged each other with their leaves and laughed. They had been telling some story or other that they found amusing. But Veronica had not heard the story, which was a good thing, because it was decidedly not a story for little girls. Radishes are usually very pert and somewhat sharp-tongued.

You couldn't possibly see and hear everything in the Garden of Spirits; there were too many voices and pictures, all drenched in shimmering light and life. It seemed to Little Veronica as if everything were turning in a circle around her, but it was well worth watching, this merry dance in a ring of bright colors.

If you only knew how soon the twilight comes, Little Veronica, you could not get enough of seeing and hearing, and you would feel you must breathe deeply into your soul all the pictures and voices in the Garden of Spirits, so that they might always be there within you. Later the world is so dark when the eyes of heaven close.

How clear and transparent everything looked now, as if the sun had pierced the Earth with light, and everything was woven of gossamer. The whole garden was full of figures. They danced in the air, and if you peered into the trees you could see elves standing in them, waving. There was rustling and whispering from every corner, and even the brightly colored pebbles moved as if they were marbles playing with themselves. And in the midst of all this glittering life, the Water-Sprite of the spring, laughing softly, suddenly showered her silver bubbles into the quivering air in a burst of fine spray. She could do this quite easily by simply spraying with her hand. You only need to have seen it once to know how wonderfully beautiful it looks.

"Would you like to play with my bright bubbles, Veronica?" called the Water-Sprite. "How would you like to have diamonds on your dress, like the King's daughter in the fairy tale? You can have all this. The fairy tale is here; we are in the Garden of Spirits."

Veronica caught one of the shining bubbles, but it dissolved in her hand. That happened because the Garden of Spirits opened off the House of Shadows; for this reason, silver fairy bubbles cannot help falling apart, because they are too close to the twilight. But Little Veronica did not know this yet.

Now she felt something tickling her bare leg. A thin feeler was reaching out as if to remind her of something.

"Wouldn't you have time now to look at my country-house?" asked the Beetle, a note of displeasure clearly audible in his faint voice. "I'm patient, it's true, but even so it has never happened to me before that someone simply sits and stares into space when she is invited to visit a country-house. Do you think it is an ordinary country-house? You won't think that any more once you have seen it."

"I beg your pardon," said Veronica, "but there's so much here to see and hear. I don't know whether I'm on my head or my heels, and everything is so lovely."

"Yes, indeed, it's very pretty," said the Beetle, "but it can't in any way be compared to my country-house. Come along with me. It's quite near here, only a few hundred steps."

"A few hundred steps is not all that near," said Veronica. "You would certainly need quite a while to crawl there. I could do it much quicker, of course."

"According to my legs, several hundred steps," said the Beetle, "measured by my legs. I measure everything only by my legs. Everyone who has any self-respect does that. One's own legs are just the things one can best rely on."

"That is just why I was thinking of my own legs and not yours," said Veronica, "and anyway, first of all I have to ask Mutzeputz if I may go and see your country-house. I never do anything without Mutzeputz."

Mutzeputz the Cat was Little Veronica's confidant, and was always near her. He strolled on velvet paws in and out between the roses and lilies, examined the cabbages and superintended the radishes. In every respect he saw to it that all was in good order. In between he played with pebbles. When they were very round he couldn't resist them. They fascinated him.

"Mutzeputz!" called Veronica. "Come here, please."

Mutzeputz the Cat never came when anyone else called him. One shouldn't let people think too much of themselves, he considered. Only when Veronica wanted him did he appear at once, because she always asked him politely, and moreover he had the firm conviction that she needed him and couldn't do anything without his advice. He felt a responsibility toward her; that was the whole point. With Mutzeputz the Cat to rely on, no one could go wrong.

With his graceful gliding movements, Mutzeputz paced at the feet of Little Veronica, and the sun streaked his soft coat with flashes of light. He was gray tiger-striped, and he wore a ceremonial white vest, with white gloves on his front paws. Again and again Veronica was filled with the thought of how un-usual Mutzeputz was, and how great a gentleman. Her hands as she stroked him were a tender caress.

"You certainly have nice acquaintances, Veron-ica!" shrieked the Blackbird from her nest, snapping her beak excitedly. "Shame on you! I wouldn't have thought you were that kind of person."

"Shut your beak!" said Mutzeputz.

"Mutzeputz," said Veronica, "the Beetle here would like to show me his country-house. Do you think I might go and see it?"

Mutzeputz looked contemptuously down at the Beetle.

"It's a harmless creature of no consequence," he said. "I don't think it's worth while to inspect his country-house. However, if it amuses you, there is no reason why you shouldn't do it. And anyway I've no time now to keep you entertained. I must go and see to things."

Mutzeputz the Cat disappeared among the rad-ishes. He lifted one with his paw and sniffed at it to ascertain whether everything was developing here as it should.

The Beetle had moved aside a little when Mutze-putz appeared. Now he approached again.

"I withdrew a bit," he explained. "I don't par-ticularly care to meet Mutzeputz."

"Mutzeputz won't do you any harm," said Ve-ronica, offended.

"No, no, certainly not," said the Beetle. "I don't want to say anything against Mutzeputz as he is close

to you and is your confidant; but there is some play-
ful quality in him, and I don't think much of being
pushed to and fro, even if it's only in fun. Who does
like that, anyway? And another thing is, my legs are
very fragile."

"Yes, they are fragile," said Veronica. "I realize
that."

"Would you like to inspect my country-house
now?" asked the Beetle.

"Yes," said Veronica. "Mutzeputz gave his permission."

"Here it is under this tree-trunk," explained the
Beetle. "It is a very beautiful country-house. It is of
somewhat light construction, to be sure, but it is only
for the summer. It wasn't too far, was it? I told you to
start with that the walk is not very tiring."

Little Veronica had only had to make one step,
and she was there.

"That wasn't a walk at all," she laughed. "It's
only next door."

"Don't give yourself airs," said the Beetle. "I
journeyed several hundred steps, so you needn't exag-
gerate. This is the entrance," he said, pointing it out.
"Then comes a small anteroom—only so big—then
my dining room, where I keep my stores too, and here
next to it is my bedchamber. It was built with special
care and the bed is made of the very best moss: you
would be hard put to it to see anything similar. This
ingenious hole in the ceiling is designed to let the sun
through. It is my custom to rest in the afternoon, and
I enjoy it above all things if the sun shines on my

back. It does so through this hole without anybody being able to see or disturb me. It is a most unusual contrivance, and as far as I know it is the first time a country-house has been equipped with it. You certainly don't have anything of the kind at home?"

"No," said Veronica. "When I'm in bed, the sun can't shine on my back, but it's all the same to me because anyway I don't lie on my tummy."

"Are you trying to make me believe that you lie on your back? If one does that, one just kicks and struggles and can't get up again. I would like you to examine the bedroom more closely and go right into it. But do be careful not to knock over my hollowed-out acorn that is standing there. I catch the dew in it and wash my face and feelers with it in the morning."

"I can look into it quite well," said Veronica, "but I can't crawl through the doorway. The whole thing is much too small for me."

"Don't lay it on so thick," said the Beetle. "Anyone would think the world was much too small for you, but the world is quite big, Little Veronica."

"Yes, it is indeed," said Veronica.

"It stretches all the way up to the great wall where there is so much moss," explained the Beetle. "However, I don't suppose you have ever been so far?"

"I have been much farther," said Veronica, "and beyond the wall there are still more things—lots and lots of things. It is a whole other world."

"These are speculations," said the Beetle. "One

can only rely on what one knows for certain. The tree elves, to be sure, say that there is a large bridge here in the garden which leads into another world. However, I have never seen such a bridge. I assume that it would be near the spring which runs through the garden. But I avoid the water and as a rule I live carefully and keep myself to myself. There are dangers and beetle-worries of various kinds in this world."

The Beetle sighed and rubbed his head uneasily with his feeler.

"I can imagine that," agreed Veronica, full of sympathy. The Beetle, in spite of his somewhat grandiose way of talking, seemed to her rather helpless. "You think, for instance, that the Blackbird who has just been shouting at me might eat you?"

"Yes, I did have such terrible things in mind," said the Beetle, "but don't talk about the Blackbird. She is an atrocious creature. I didn't know you had such shocking acquaintances. Otherwise I hardly think I would have shown you my country-house."

" I only know the Blackbird very slightly," apologized Veronica, "and she scolds me because I am friends with Mutzeputz, and now you scold me because I know the Blackbird. What is the matter with you all?"

"I am not saying anything against Mutzeputz," said the Beetle, "but the Blackbird is quite a dangerous person. Just ask the earthworms about it. They are entirely of the same opinion, and they are certainly people of experience."

"There are earthworms here too?" asked Veronica, looking around. "I think earthworms are rather nasty; they are so long and naked. Brrr!"

"They are quiet and pleasant neighbors," said the Beetle. "I would be only too pleased if everyone were like them. Unfortunately, this is not the case. You wouldn't believe it, but one hardly gets the necessary amount of peace and quiet in one's own country-house. I don't want to say anything derogatory about the spirits who look after the growth of the plants, although they are busybodies and on the go the whole time—too much so, if you ask me. One has to admit that they work silently and with a great deal of consideration for other people. Only once did a root grow straight through my anteroom, and we came to an agreement to widen it so that I could use it as a hammock. However, if one looks deeper into the Earth, it's enough to make one furious. Anger is very bad for me; it gives me a headache immediately. Down there are the real disturbers of the peace. They are tiny black and white dwarfs, with your kind of shape but much uglier. You won't believe it how these dwarfs quarrel. I hear it often at night; it comes all the way up to my bedroom. They are an abominable crowd. If you could only see them!"

"I would like to see them," said Veronica. "I wish you would show them to me. It must be terribly funny to see them quarrel among themselves. And why do they quarrel? After all, one can't quarrel all the time. I quarrel sometimes with Peter when we are playing, but we always make it up right away. Peter is the gardener's son. As you know, his father runs the whole garden here."

"That is nonsense," said the Beetle. "Nobody runs the garden. Everything grows here quite by itself, and in any case it was always here."

"You don't know then why the dwarfs quarrel?" asked Veronica. It didn't seem to her any good to explain to the Beetle who the gardener was.

"I did hear it once, but I forgot it again," said the Beetle. "I always get a headache when I think of it. It will give you a headache too, so let it be and don't bother about it."

"I never get headaches," said Veronica. "Only grownups get headaches, and then they are horrid and you are not allowed to ask them anything. And it doesn't bother me a bit either if the dwarfs quarrel. Why should it matter? It's all the same to me. I only want to see it sometime because it must be a lot of fun."

"You will get headaches when you are older," said the Beetle, "and it is a matter of concern to all of us when the dwarfs quarrel. That is what the Tree Elf told me, and she knows all about it. You see, from her house you can look past the roots straight down to the dwarfs."

"That's wonderful," said Veronica. "Then I will ask the Tree Elf if I may have a really good look at the whole thing. Do you think the Elf would let me do that? She ought to be a good friend of yours if you are such close neighbors?"

"We are not exactly good friends," said the

Beetle. "This would not be in keeping with proper re-spect, if I may express myself in this way. You must know that I am under the protection of the Tree Elf, so to speak. She doesn't allow the Blackbird to come and eat me, and one way and another she takes care that nothing untoward befalls me. That is why I stay close to my country-house all the time. There are so many dangers and all kinds of beetle-worries in this world. But I am sure you could go in and see the Tree Elf. She is really very obliging. You simply have to slip through the bark. There she is sitting inside; don't you see?"

"Come, Little Veronica," called the Elf, looking out of her tree. She was a lovely creature, and looked like a delicately made young girl who had never grown big.

"But I can't get in there," said Veronica.

"Now I want to go and lie on my stomach in my bedroom and get some rest," said the Beetle, "so that the sun can shine on my back through this ingenious hole. It is quite out of the ordinary, this device; you can look at it again later on. Now I will bid you good-day."

"You can reach me in the tree quite well, Little Veronica," said the Tree Elf, "only not quite as you are now. You will have to change a little and slip out of your body."

"That sounds rather uncomfortable, and I've never tried it. Besides, my body is not a dress that I can just take off. What would I walk about in without it? Wouldn't it be enough if I looked into your roots and down to the dwarfs the same way I looked at the Beetle's house? That worked very well, and I would have seen much more still if the Beetle hadn't chattered so much. And then he insists that *he* has a headache!"

"The Beetle is a bit fussy," said the Elf in the tree, laughing. "Small people with lots of legs are mostly that way. But you cannot look into my home here the same way you looked into the Beetle's house. It is true you still have the eyes of heaven, Little Veronica, and with them you can see many things above the Earth and on it. But to see into the depths you must have other eyes. That takes a long time, and it is very painful. You had better slip in here close to me, because you can still do that quite well. The twilight has not overtaken you yet, Little Veronica. And you need not be afraid. Your earthly body is after all nothing more than a dress, and inside it is a finer dress, and you yourself are in this finer dress. You can quite well leave the coarse earthly dress by itself for a while where it is. Inside the finer dress you are just like me and all the elves and fairies in the water, in the air and in the fire. You only have to give yourself a push, just as you do before going to sleep—it's almost the same—and then it goes by itself."

Then Veronica gave herself a push, and suddenly she was outside, as light as a feather when the wind plays with it and so transparent that she could look through herself. Her earthly body sat beside her, looking rather silly, she thought. The next moment she was in the middle of the tree and the Elf had taken her by the hands and was showing her all the wonders inside.

There was a lot to see, much more than in the Beetle's country-house, and Veronica's amazement never ceased. The sap rose and fell in a thousand fine veins, from the roots to the highest tip, and far into the branches and leaves moving gently in the wind. And the beauty of it was that you were part of it, rising and falling as if in a living swing.

"Now that I am in it, I can understand everything much better than before when I could only look into it from outside," said Veronica. "It seems as if I had become much cleverer altogether, now that I'm no longer stuck in my earthly body. I believe it makes you a bit stupid, and certainly very much heavier, because it's really marvelous how light I am now."

"Yes, indeed," said the Elf, "you all get rather stupid on account of your earthly bodies. And they are such uncomfortable dresses—I wouldn't be able to move around in them. The worst of it is that the larger the earthly body gets and the more you grow into it, the stupider you become. I can only imagine how you feel, because I have not gone through it all myself."

"Do we come to Earth so as to grow stupid?" asked Veronica. "That seems sort of funny to me, you know."

"That isn't it," said the Elf. "You only become stupid because it gets dark, and then you should look for the light so that you may become wise again. Because when you have found the light in the darkness, then you have become a great deal wiser. To seek the light is truly the task of human beings, imposed on them by God. They must seek it out and find it, not only for themselves, but for the animals, the plants, and the stones, for the elves and dwarfs, for every being that lives with them. That is rather a difficult story though, and I cannot explain it to you exactly."

"It sounds very difficult to me," said Veronica. "Couldn't God arrange it a little more conveniently and simply? It must be easy enough for Him. After all, He can do just as He likes. I'll ask Him about it when I meet Him. But it's probably not easy to get to talk to Him. He must have a lot to do?"

"Oh, Little Veronica," said the Elf with a sigh, "if you seek God you will have to travel many difficult roads, and when you find Him at last you will no longer ask Him what you asked today. To seek God and to find God—that is more than a child's question. If it were not so, maybe all of us would have found deliverance."

"Are you bewitched, then?" asked Veronica. "That sounds like Snow White in the fairy tale."

"In the fairy tale everything is as real as it is on Earth," said the Elf. "Oh, if human beings would only understand this!"

"Snow White is asleep in the glass coffin," said Veronica softly, and a solemn, faraway look came into her eyes.

The Elf took Veronica by the hand.

"We are all asleep in the glass coffin," she said. "Remember this; remember it always when you grow up, Little Veronica. Yes, help us in the task of deliverance—of you and of us all. But that is so very difficult, Little Veronica. Today you cannot yet understand it."

"Why not?" asked Veronica. "Didn't I grow cleverer when I slipped out of my earthly body?"

"Maybe," said the Elf, "but not wise enough yet. In order to bring about deliverance you have to get into the glass coffin yourself and go deep into the darkness, until you find the light. But all human beings have to do that—the other creatures are waiting for it so eagerly."

"I would have arranged that more simply if I were God," Veronica said thoughtfully.

"Do you think it would have been just as good?" asked the Elf.

"I don't know about that, of course," said Veronica. "I can't take it all in. But I think it's important for us and Snow White to get out of the glass coffin. I'll think it over a bit more later on: at the moment it seems very difficult. But won't you show me the dwarfs quarreling? It would be such fun."

"Come," said the Elf, "you must look here through the roots. The little dwarfs are deep down in the Earth under the roots. Can you see them? There are only two there. From here you can't see everything that happens down below in the Earth."

"Oh, yes, there they are! They do look funny!" cried Veronica, bending down. "One is black and the other white, and they are both as small as mice. Now the black dwarf is jumping at the white one and try-

ing to snatch a stone from him. That's a pretty stone
—and look, the white dwarf has a hammer in his
hand, with sparks sputtering out of it! Oh, how wonderful that looks! But the black one is frightfully angry, and now they are quarreling. Tell me, what are
they trying to do with the stone?"

"Well, you see, Veronica," said the Elf, "the
white dwarf chips stones into a beautiful shape and
he wants to get the sparks into the stone so that the
light goes through it. There are clear stones too, you
know, and that is how the whole Earth should be
lighted from within. But the black dwarfs don't want
that to happen."

"Why ever not?" asked Veronica. "It would look
wonderfully pretty."

"Certainly," said the Elf, "and everything would
then become quite light and transparent: people, animals, plants—not only stones."

"That ought to be done," said Veronica. "It
would be lovely if you could look into everybody and
see what is inside."

"When you are older, Little Veronica," said the
Elf, "you will realize that people are not at all anxious
for others to look inside them. And you will understand why, because human beings keep inside them
some very ugly and terrible things. As to the black
dwarfs, they wouldn't allow anyone to look into them,
because what is inside *them* is truly horrible. That is
why they want everything on Earth to be as black
and dark as they are themselves."

"I don't think we should stand for it," said Veronica. "They are only mice on two legs; what do they have to say about anything? Couldn't we just give them a little push? It's quite easy."

"Neither of us can do that," said the Elf. "Neither I nor you, Veronica. At least not yet. And listen, even if you push a black dwarf aside—and you will often do this later on—there are many, many more of them, and behind them stand great and powerful figures. If you could see them, you would no longer talk of mice."

"Oh, do please show me!" cried Veronica, clapping her hands excitedly. "There is such a lot to see with you. I'll have to visit you quite often in the tree."

"Who knows when you will come back, Little Veronica?" said the Elf. "Perhaps the twilight will soon come down on you, and you will forget me and all these things for quite a while. Anyway, I am not allowed to show you the great ones. It would give you such a fright that you wouldn't be able to slip back into your earthly dress. But that is just what you must do, because your journey is only now beginning."

"Must I make a journey?" asked Veronica. "I only go for walks in the garden as I did today."

"You will make many journeys, and they won't be just walks, Little Veronica."

"Oh, do you think so?" said Veronica. "And do the same kind of great ones stand behind the white dwarfs too? Oh, look how the dwarfs are quarreling! But the white one has managed to keep hold of the stone after all. I'm so glad. Now he ought to be able to make it beautifully clear and transparent."

"Yes, behind the white dwarfs stand great ones too. But they are not horrible; they are wonderfully beautiful. So beautiful, though, that you couldn't bear it. You must wait, Little Veronica, until you have the eyes of the depths; then you will be able to see both."

"Then I wish I could have the eyes of the depths very soon," said Veronica with longing.

"Oh, Little Veronica, don't wish that! The eyes of the depths grow through tears, and the tears will come soon enough."

There was a light tapping on the tree trunk. Outside stood a sylph, looking as if woven entirely from bright colors, with butterfly wings on his shoulders.

"Oh, isn't he pretty!" cried Veronica.

"I have been told to call for Little Veronica and take her to the Silver Bridge again," he said softly.

"That's nice of you," said Veronica. "How exciting! I'd love to see a silver bridge."

"I believe your twilight is nearly here, Veronica," said the Elf. "Climb up to the tree-top; then the Sylph will take your hand, and you will fly with him to the Silver Bridge."

"Aren't you coming?" said Veronica. "Do come too. We had such a nice talk."

"No, I can't come with you," said the Elf. "I am tied to the tree and must stay in it until it dies or is cut down. That will happen one day."

"Oh," said Veronica sadly, "does that hurt very much?"

"Yes, it hurts," said the Elf, "but not in the way you think. It is like moving out of a house you have become attached to and going to another one—not like cutting your finger. We don't feel that kind of hurt. And we don't die like human beings and animals, because they have grown into their earthly body in a different way, and it is a greater break for them when they leave it and go over the Silver Bridge. But we are different. We are half at home here and half there, until all of us find the same home. But that will only happen when Snow White has awakened."

"I can't quite understand it all," said Veronica, "and I've never died and never moved from one house to another."

"You have done both things many times already," said the Sylph from above, "only you forgot them again. The twilight came in between, and now it will soon come back, Little Veronica. But first we still have to fly to the Silver Bridge."

Then the Elf lifted Veronica and carried her high into the top of the tree where the Sylph was waiting for her.

"Good-bye, Little Veronica," she said. "Don't forget me. But I know as a matter of fact that you will forget me when the twilight comes. So I would rather say: think of me again another time, and then remember that Snow White is asleep in the glass coffin just as we all are, and that all of us await our deliverance."

"Yes, I will think of it," promised Veronica. "Good-bye for now. I'll come back soon."

"You won't come so soon, and when you walk once more through the Garden of Spirits, much will have happened, Veronica," called the Elf after her and waved her hand in farewell.

Overhead in the green branches sat the Blackbird, making a lot of noise.

"You need not shout so," said Veronica. "I was angry with you because you scolded me for being friends with Mutzeputz. Mutzeputz is much cleverer than you, and I never do anything without asking him. What's more, I want to tell you that you have no reason to be abusive about other people, because the Beetle told me worse things about you than you did about Mutzeputz. The Beetle said you were an atrocious creature, and the earthworms think so too. The Beetle said he wouldn't have shown me his country-house if he had known that I knew you. You see, that's what I think of you, and you have no right to insult Mutzeputz. Anyway, Mutzeputz always has his meals regularly, so he doesn't need to eat you. *You* least of all!"

It was a relief to Veronica to get this off her chest, because she couldn't bear it when people didn't show due respect to Mutzeputz. But the Blackbird sat there with her beak wide open at such appalling insolence. Really no one had ever said anything of this kind to her before, and the worst of it was that there was nothing one could contradict in it.

"You are quite right, Veronica," said the Sylph. "But listen, Mutzeputz is right, and the Blackbird, and the Beetle, and the earthworms as well. There are forces which destroy them, because these creatures have to go down into the twilight, and this will only change when Snow White wakes up again. You can contribute something to it, and so can all other human beings. These are great secrets of coming into being and of passing away, Veronica, only today they are a little too difficult for you. But surely you can understand that you wouldn't like it if anyone tried to eat you—not *you*, of course, but your earthly body?"

"Yes," said Veronica; "I've never been eaten, so I can't say anything about it. But I imagine it would be horrid."

"You see," said the Sylph. "And now try to imagine someone coming and eating up those you love—you do have loved ones, don't you?"

"Of course," said Veronica eagerly. "Mutzeputz and Mama, Uncle Johannes, Aunt Mariechen, Peter, and my dolls—no, no one is allowed to eat them, that would be awful. Caroline shouldn't be eaten, either. Caroline is the cook, you know. She talks very loudly, but Mutzeputz thinks a lot of her. It's rather funny that he does, because he generally doesn't like to be talked to in a loud voice. We talk to each other mostly with our thoughts. Nobody can eat Papa now, because he is in heaven. Mama says God needed him badly for some reason, and we have to look after ourselves without him."

"Do you love Mutzeputz most of all, Veronica," asked the Sylph, "as you mentioned him first?"

"I love everybody," said Veronica, "but I thought of Mutzeputz first because I always ask him about everything. You can't ask the others at all in the same way because they don't understand everything you say. Uncle Johannes is the best, and he may even be just as wise as Mutzeputz, though I don't really think so. Anyway, both of them are great friends of mine, and Uncle Johannes thinks a lot of Mutzeputz."

"Uncle Johannes is absolutely right," said the Sylph, "but now let us fly together to the Silver Bridge."

"How can I do that?" asked Veronica nervously. "I would have to have beautiful wings like yours."

"You have them. Don't you feel how they have grown onto your shoulders? That happens quickly with us in the Garden of Spirits."

And indeed, Veronica felt softly fluttering butterfly wings move on her shoulders, and she glided effortlessly with the Sylph from the top of the tree into the wide, sun-filled summer air.

Butterflies flew all around her. "Now you are like us, Veronica," they said.

Far below them lay the garden with cabbages and radishes, with flowers, beetles, and earthworms, and the Water-Sprite threw her bright bubbles into the blue air so that they burst in the sunlight like a thousand sparkling diamonds.

"Why do you fly so high over the garden, Veronica?" asked the Hedgehog mother. "First you should look how beautifully my children roll themselves together."

"Oh, the dear little balls, full of prickles!" she cried, enchanted.

"How dare you talk of balls?" said the Hedgehog mother angrily. "Balls indeed! These are my children. What would you think if I called your children balls? And anyway, what kind of talk is this?"

"Everyone takes offense very easily around here," said Veronica. "First the Blackbird scolds, then the Beetle, and now the Hedgehog. And this was after I said how enchanting her children were!"

"The deeper you go in the garden of the Earth, the more everything is misunderstood; that is because of the twilight, Veronica, and human beings most of all misunderstand and become abusive," said the Sylph.

"Veronica didn't mean it that way," he called down. "And besides, a ball is the most perfect of all shapes."

"Really? Is that true?" asked the Hedgehog mother, flattered. "And where are you flying in such a hurry?"

"Across the spring to the Silver Bridge," called the Sylph.

"That is where I want to go too," said the Hedgehog mother. "But how shall I get over the water with the little ones? I have been looking for a suitable crossing for a long time."

"At the other end of the garden is a little bridge," said the Sylph. "It crosses the spring."

"Always these roundabout ways," growled the Hedgehog mother. "No, that is too difficult for me today. Then we had better stay here. It's nice and sunny here today."

"Yes, one has to go a roundabout way to get to the Silver Bridge," said the Sylph, "and you will still have to make quite a few detours of this kind, Little Veronica. But for the Hedgehog it is far too early yet, and she still has work to do here. And anyway, she is still too sensitive and touchy."

"If the Silver Bridge is on the other side of the spring, it must be where Uncle Johannes lives," said Veronica. "Perhaps he even built it himself? If so, he might have told me about it."

"Uncle Johannes has already built a good many bridges which lead to the Silver Bridge, but he cannot build the Silver Bridge itself. More likely he built his home there because he discovered the Silver Bridge next to it," said the Sylph. "Look, Veronica, here it is."

The Silver Bridge rose on silver columns from the Garden of Spirits. It ascended in a wide arc into the clear air and lost itself in the shimmering sunlight in a splendor unendurable to the eye. Veronica had never seen anything so beautiful. But at the same time she felt quite at home here, and as if she had often walked over the Silver Bridge. But when could that have been—when? She could not remember at all. Where the bridge began, the earth and the stones were as clear as glass, and around them bloomed lilies and roses filled with light, and a thousand other flowers that Veronica did not know. Noiseless and weightless, forms of human beings and animals flowed over the bridge, and they too were shot through with that light which illuminated the flowers and the stones. In the middle of the bridge, however, just at the place where it lost itself in splendor, were only angels with silver wings, robed in white. Veronica had become absolutely still, and was conscious of nothing but the light in herself. At the same time she felt that she had to look at one angel in particular above all the others, perhaps because he, too, had his eyes on her.

"Look at the Silver Bridge, Little Veronica; you came from it and you will return to it," said the white-clad Angel. "But first comes the twilight."

Little Veronica was then gripped by a great fear of the twilight, although she did not quite know what it was.

"Don't be afraid, Little Veronica," said the Angel. "The twilight will come, and the splendor of the Silver Bridge will fade. And, too, the Garden of Spirits will no longer look as you saw it today for the last time. It will be very dark when the twilight comes. But I will go with you, and I will light your three candles for you, Little Veronica, and will watch over you."

A great gray veil fell over the Silver Bridge and over everything on it, so that Veronica could no longer see anything there. There was a deep silence and sadness around her. Only from far away soft voices sounded.

"See how white our blossoms are," said the Lily spirits. "So pure and so white is the heavenly garment you will wear again one day."

"Look how red our cups are," said the Rosesouls. "So pure and so red is the chalice of the Grail to which you will once more stretch out your arms."

The gray veil darkened, and now it covered the Garden of Spirits too, so that Veronica could no longer see as clearly as before.

The Sylph held out his hand to her.

"Good-bye, Veronica," said he.

"Are you leaving me too?" asked Veronica. "Don't go. I'm afraid to be left alone."

"You won't be alone," said the Sylph, and his radiant colors seemed to fade. "Your Angel will watch over you, and after all you have Mutzeputz and the others whom you can ask for advice."

"I would still like to have someone like you, or the Elf in the tree," said Veronica.

"You will have that too when you enter the House of Shadows," said the Sylph, with a kind smile. "In the House of Shadows lives a little creature who is closely related to us. He is called Master Mützchen, and he will take care of you in every way he can."

"Master Mützchen?" repeated Veronica. "What a funny name!"

"Perhaps you would like to look at my country-house?" again asked a small, faint beetle-voice from very far away and scarcely audible.

Then darkness fell over the Garden of Spirits. The eyes of heaven had closed.

*

"Veronica!" called someone. It was her mother's voice.

"Yes, Mama, I'm coming!"

And with a push that hurt a bit, Little Veronica slipped back into her earthly body. Her mother stood looking at her.

"Have you been asleep, Veronica?" she asked gently.

"No, Mama, I wasn't asleep; I was wide awake and I was with the Beetle and the Tree Elf, and afterwards the Sylph showed me the Silver Bridge."

"You have been dreaming, Veronica."

"Oh no, it was all very real," said Veronica, and it grieved her to think that grownups could never understand what was much more real than the whole world.

But when she tried to remember everything exactly herself, she could not do it any longer. Only a glimmering was there, but it wouldn't come clear.

The great twilight had begun.

"Come, Veronica," said her mother. "Take your spade and pail, and you can go on digging your flowerbed tomorrow. Now we must go home. Where is Mutzeputz, by the way?"

When Mutzeputz heard his name, he came bounding up to Veronica and her mother, ran ahead of them, and sprang over the steps onto the porch to wait there. In no circumstances did he want Veronica's mother to think he had come only because she had called him. After all, one has to preserve one's independence if one is Mutzeputz the Cat.

"How dark the garden has grown, and it was so light," thought Veronica. "I can't see anything clearly any more."

But it was not really too bad, and Little Veronica could still see quite a lot of things. At the top of the steps stood a tiny creature with thin legs, dressed in a gray coat and wearing a pointed red hat on his head. He was no bigger than the span of two hands, extremely agile, and altogether very comical. How odd that Mama didn't see him! At least she didn't say anything.

Veronica laughed, and suddenly she remembered what the Sylph had told her when he said good-bye.

"Are you Master Mützchen?" she asked.

"At your service! Mützchen, Master Mützchen, at your service," said the little creature, bowing continuously.

Then he took the red hat from his head and held it in front of his body. Betweenwhiles he made grimaces that were really something to see. He came up the steps with them.

"Don't fall, Little Veronica," he said, and took her by the hand.

This gave Veronica a great feeling of calm, and she knew she had found a good companion.

"Is it so easy to fall here?" she asked, and this time she spoke aloud and not only in her thoughts.

"Many have already fallen over these steps, Little Veronica," said Master Mützchen. "Oh, so many! This is the House of Shadows you are going into, and it has many steps and thresholds."

"Who are you talking to, Veronica?" asked her mother.

"Oh, nobody," said Veronica.

Then they all went into the House of Shadows.

That night Little Veronica could not sleep for a long time. She lay in bed with open eyes and looked at Mutzeputz who slept at her feet, and at Master Mützchen who was doing gymnastics on the bedpost and making unbelievable faces. You couldn't help admiring the way he did it.

"Be a little quiet," said Veronica, "so that Mama doesn't wake up."

"She won't wake up," said Master Mützchen. "She's fast asleep, and she wouldn't see me anyway. But I won't go on fooling; someone else is coming to you."

Suddenly it grew very light in the room, and Veronica saw that the Angel from the Silver Bridge was standing by her bed. Veronica recognized him immediately, and a great and joyful peace came over her.

"How lovely that you have come," she said. "I have been a bit worried. I feel as if I had been through a lot today and as if something special had happened."

"That is true, Veronica," said the Angel, and looked at Little Veronica with great love in his eyes. "Today you have seen the Garden of Spirits and the Silver Bridge for the last time in a long while, and the eyes of heaven have closed..Now they will only be able to see in the House of Shadows. The great twilight has come, and now your journey is beginning. But you must not be afraid when it is dark. I will light your three candles and watch over you and them."

"Oh, please, watch over Mutzeputz and Master Mützchen and the others as well," pleaded Veronica.

"Yes," said the Angel. "I will also watch over Mutzeputz and Master Mützchen. Over the others too, if they want to be watched over. But it is not all human beings who want that the way you think they do."

Calmly and ceremoniously the Angel placed a large, curiously wrought, three-branched candlestick in front of Veronica. At the end of each branch burned a small flame—a blue one and a red one at the sides, and a golden one a little higher in the middle.

"Now your three candles are burning in the twilight," said the Angel. "Blessings on your journey, Little Veronica!"

Veronica looked wide-eyed at the light of the flames and at the Angel. She saw that Master Mützchen was sitting reverently in a corner, and she heard Mutzeputz purring softly. Then an infinite tiredness came over her and she fell asleep.

But the Angel remained at her bedside and kept his hand over the three candles of Little Veronica.

CHAPTER II

THE HOUSE OF SHADOWS

HE next morning, Little Veronica felt as if she had slept very deeply, and it seemed much more than a single night between yesterday and today. It was as though she had been born into a new life in a new world. This was because for the first time she was fully awake in the House of Shadows. It is true she had already been living in the House of Shadows, but more in the body than in the soul. In the Garden of Spirits she had really lived, but in the House of Shadows she had been going around only half aware—it had been for her only something transitory, and she did not feel part of it. Now that the twilight had actually come, the Garden of Spirits had disappeared behind the veil and the House of Shadows entered into her consciousness. That is one of the thresholds in human existence, and we must all cross it. But people forget it all; they forget that they were ever in the Garden of Spirits, and smile in unbelief if they are told about it. And many forget too about their experiences later in the House of Shadows, and think that in the whole of human existence the only real things are those which can be touched and belong to this world alone. But true life plays its ever-changing game in all the variety of its colors behind these tangible things, and destiny weaves its invisible threads between the Garden of Spirits and the House of Shadows with its multitude of strange pictures. Everyone must guard within his soul a little of the Garden of Spirits and of the House of Shadows, other-wise later on he will not find his way aright amidst the perplexities of existence. And each must remem-ber his three candles on the altar of life, or he will trip over the many steps and thresholds which he cannot see in the dark.

For every house is a House of Shadows, and it was not only Little Veronica who lived in a House of Shadows. We all live in one, wherever we might be on this Earth, and we all pass over steps and thresh-olds we cannot see and which are lighted only by an inner light. It is hard to cross over thresholds and steps, and it is sad to live in Houses of Shadows—perhaps worst of all for those who are not aware of it.

It has not always been so. There was a time—spoken of in old legends and fairy tales—when people lived in temples and in light-filled mansions. That was in the Morningland of Mankind; but afterwards men climbed down into the dark, and out of their deeds wove destinies and built Houses of Shadows. All you who walk the Earth today live in them, and of a cer-tainty it is often hard and oppressive to live there. But you must not let this sadden you. Remember the small flames that light you all, as the three candles of Little Veronica lighted her—remember them, you who walk the Earth today. Cast their light clear through your Houses of Shadows. Then once more you will be living in temples and in light-filled mansions.

There are indeed long roads from one far place to another. But do not think you have traveled them in vain. It was not you who built the temples and the mansions full of light where you lived in the Morningland of Mankind—you lived in them just as children do in the Garden of Spirits. But you yourselves will have built the new temples and the new mansions that will grow out of the Houses of Shadows; you will have built them with your own thoughts, and in them you will experience the consciousness of a child. Conscious childhood is blessedness. For this, is it not worth while to cross many steps and thresholds, even if it is a long road from one far place to another?

We come from distant heights, and to a far-off land we make our homeward journey. Build your temples, all you who walk the Earth today; build your mansions. Fill them with light.

Little Veronica did not know any of this on awakening in the House of Shadows. She was still so young; how should she know? Perhaps she guessed it, for her three candles were burning and her Angel was holding his hand over them. She herself did not think about it any more, and saw nothing, because it is not always that we see our Angel and the three flames which light us.

But now Little Veronica became aware of quantities of new things in the House of Shadows. It seemed to her as if she had awakened in it for the first time, and as if there were opening before her eyes a new world with a mass of confusing corridors and mysterious doors. It is true that the eyes of heaven which saw so clearly in the Garden of Spirits had closed, but now beginning to open were those other eyes which could see the thresholds and steps in the House of Shadows. This is a first small indication of what the eyes of the depths are. But for most people these eyes fall asleep again, and so they do not understand life, for life lies behind things, and its path is elusive.

What a number of steps and thresholds Little Veronica saw! You couldn't rush through the rooms as easily and unhampered as before, when you had lived there still only half aware. But she quite quickly became used to it. If you took care, all went well, and you could easily skip over things along the way. But when the steps were steep and high, you were more inclined to walk around them. With great skill Mutzeputz and Master Mützchen vaulted over them, making light of it as if it were nothing at all or as if they were having fun slipping under them. To be sure, we have to consider that for Mutzeputz and Master Mützchen the steps and thresholds are far less dangerous and important than for a human child, the threads of whose destiny can only too easily become entangled with them and lead to downfall.

By the way, Mutzeputz and Master Mützchen got

on splendidly together. It was as if they had known each other for a long time, and as a matter of fact that is just what it was, for both had lived in the House of Shadows far longer than had Little Veronica in her new awareness. After all, this had only begun last night when her three candles were lighted. As far as Master Mützchen was concerned, it could be taken more or less for granted that he had already been living here for hundreds of years, and when he hopped around all over on his thin, dusty legs, he often looked as if he had come out of the old brickwork, and his little coat and breeches seemed to be made of gray spiderweb. Only the red hat exercised a striking effect of its own, and showed that the wearer must indeed be a creature in his own right. He had grown very intimate with the House of Shadows; he knew exactly where all the hiding places were and pointed out every single thing worth seeing like an experienced guide. How clearly, for instance, he could explain that the woodworm in the old cupboard was meticulous in working to a very special, eminently pleasing pattern —how precisely he could prove why the spider had spun her web exactly in that corner over there, why a mousehole must be just here, and there a weak place in the wall.

He showed Veronica all the many rooms and corridors, and she saw them as if for the first time, for up to now she had only been in them, she had not experienced them. Now, however, she noticed that they were all different: in one it was warm and light, even when the shutters were closed, for it had an inner

lightness. In another room, though, it felt chilly even
in the heat of summer, and it was dark there even
when the sunshine flooded it. At any rate, you felt
this so clearly that there could not be any doubt. It
was the same thing with the furniture and with the
pictures. They too were light or dark, warm or cold,
and there were things among them that you felt you
would rather not touch. Besides, near these things
there were always an extra lot of steps. How strange
it all was!

But oddest of all it seemed to Little Veronica
that she was no longer as free as she had been before
in the Garden of Spirits, where you could hear so
many voices and see so many pictures and could always choose for yourself just wherever you felt like
going. In the House of Shadows, however, you continu-
ally felt as if you were being nudged a little, not phys-
ically, but nevertheless very noticeably. Of course,
you did not always have to give way, but you did it
only too easily, for that is what follows if you are
tapped suddenly on the shoulder and nudged along.
Often, too, Veronica noticed that Master Mützchen
diverted her when something tried to draw her away
in this fashion. You couldn't see anyone doing it; you
could only feel it as you feel currents in a river where
you are swimming. It was quite fun to be touched and
gently nudged here and there—it was exciting and
just like one invitation after another. You yourself
didn't really want to—something in you wanted to.
And then everywhere there was something to see.

But it will not always be such fun to be nudged

along, Little Veronica. You will be drawn over many steep and toilsome steps, and forced over many thresholds that terrify you.

One day Veronica felt again that she was touched lightly on the shoulder and drawn along. She followed through several rooms and corridors, in which Master Mützchen hopped around her a little anxiously. It was as if he wanted to hold her back, for ever and again he jumped in the way, but evidently he could not conquer it—there were powerful forces in the House of Shadows. Who knew that better than Master Mützchen? He had lived here for hundreds of years.

Little Veronica walked through the long, somewhat gloomy gallery, which was seldom used and where antique furniture stood, stiff and ceremonious; and now there was a door in front of her through which she had never been before. The door was ajar, and it did not look as if there were anyone in the room beyond. Veronica's heart began to pound; she didn't know why. She was not really frightened.

"Something is pushing me in there in an extraordinary way," she said, looking at Master Mützchen. She couldn't ask Mutzeputz's advice just then. He was detained on business and was around somewhere, seeing to it that everything was in order.

"This is the Green Room," explained Master Mützchen. "There are a great many pictures there, but no one in the house likes it. It would be better, Veronica, if you didn't walk over this threshold yet. Mutzeputz, too, thoroughly disapproves of this room;

he has been most critical of it. Indeed, I heard him say once that even the mice had moved out of it. I don't want to explain in detail. It would be better if we went along to your dolls and you introduced me to them."

But Little Veronica felt herself strangely drawn to the Green Room. Cautiously she opened the door a little wider and slipped inside.

The shutters were closed, and you had to get used to the semidarkness. Fitful threads of sunlight spun themselves through the half-light; they flashed here and there on the polished bronze fittings and the green brocade of the furniture, or dappled the faded colors of old pictures. A great many pictures hung on the walls—men and women in all sorts of different costume were there, and all of them looked at Veronica. It was a little uncomfortable here.

"We ought to be leaving now," urged Master Mützchen, tugging at Veronica's dress.

But it was too late to go.

"Good day, Veronica," said a voice behind her.

Veronica looked around. A young, beautiful woman stood in front of her, but this was not a real woman such as she usually saw. It was as if she were made of gray smoke, and as Veronica looked she noticed that this was the same lovely woman as the one in the picture before which she was standing. But now the woman was without any of the colors she had in the painting.

Veronica was a little frightened, but not really badly. It did not strike her as any stranger than Mas-

ter Mützchen or all the steps and thresholds she saw.
All told, she had a good many aunts. Why shouldn't
this be another one, who was a bit transparent and
misty? She looked friendly too, and certainly there
was no need to be frightened.

"It's charming of you to come and visit me, Little Veronica," said the Gray Lady, smiling. It was a
pretty, winning smile, exactly the way the old picture
in the gilt frame smiled. A smile not easy to forget.

Veronica took a liking to this aunt. Besides, she
was so amusingly dressed, quite different for instance
from Mama or Aunt Mariechen.

"Was it you who tugged me, so I had to come
here?" asked Veronica.

"It was not I, but something of me that drew you
in," said the Gray Lady. "I wanted very much to
know you better. We are really relations, Little Veronica."

"Oh," said Veronica, not too politely, and looked
very closely at the Gray Lady. She was a real aunt
then, and there were different aunts, the ones with
colors and the gray ones, the solid and the misty. It
was a good thing to know about this.

"Don't fall, Little Veronica; there are so many
steps and thresholds here," said the Gray Lady, sitting
down in an old high-backed chair. "You can watch
everything here if it amuses you, but you must be a
little careful."

"I take good care," said Veronica. "Master Mützchen is with me too, and looks after me, so nothing
can happen to me."

Master Mützchen ran busily here and there, waving his thin arms frantically.

"Ah, Little Veronica, Master Mützchen can't help you forever," sighed the Lady.

"Why do you shut yourself up here in the Green Room? Isn't it boring?" asked Veronica. "I haven't seen you anywhere else. Don't you ever walk through the house or in the garden?"

"It's a long time since I went out, Veronica."

"You must go for walks more; it's not good for you to sit all the time in a musty room," said Veronica, feeling very clever at giving the misty aunt advice.

"I could go out, Veronica, but I always have to come back. I must manage to cross this one threshold, you see, and I can't do it. No, I simply can't!"

The Gray Lady in the armchair shrank into herself, and her face took on such a tormented look that Veronica was truly sorry for her.

"I can't see anything special about this threshold you are pointing to. It is not so high and dreadful as you think. Watch how I jump over it!"

"Don't do that, Veronica," called Master Mützchen. "You shouldn't go over this threshold any more now, otherwise you will slip back into the Garden of Spirits and to the Silver Bridge. You have only just come from there, and it would be too soon to turn back again today. You must be patient now and stay quite some time in the House of Shadows. There are many other steps and thresholds you must go over in the future."

Veronica obediently came back from the threshold.

"Ought the gray aunt to go over it?"

"She ought to, but she can't," said Master Mützchen softly. "Her case is a bit different; she has already been too long in the House of Shadows."

An odd shudder came over Veronica. The Green Room struck her as colder and darker than all the others.

"I wouldn't like to be so much alone here as you," she said. The Gray Lady shook her head.

"I am not lonely, Veronica; there are plenty of others here. Look!"

A ghostly blue light crept slowly along the walls; it filled the whole place, and now Veronica saw that the Gray Lady was no longer alone. In all the chairs sat figures in old-fashioned costume like the Gray Lady's dress. But they did not speak, and moved with strange noiselessness, like puppets. Many of them bore a great resemblance to the pictures on the wall, and a slim young man with a tricorn hat and sword reminded Veronica a little of Uncle Johannes. But he was different. And how should Uncle Johannes be here among all these strange people? Probably he was now sitting reading in his garden house. Furthermore, it was not he at all—yet Veronica was impelled to think about him.

The various figures who were now sitting in the chairs did not seem as real to Veronica as the Gray Lady. True, the gray aunt was also a little misty and out of the ordinary. But she was there, and you could

talk to her. The others, on the other hand, looked as
if they had been painted with faded washed-out
strokes in empty space. Nevertheless, the Gray Lady
nodded now to this, now to that, apparition and made
as if to speak to each. She was completely occupied
with this and did not look at Veronica any more.

All at once Veronica felt icy cold. A feeling of
horror seized her; she ran out of the door and pulled
it shut behind her.

Beside her stood Master Mützchen.

"You see," said he disapprovingly, "that's no
company for you, Veronica."

"I didn't know this kind of people lived here,"
said Veronica. "Are they really alive? It didn't look
like it."

"Only the Gray Lady is alive," said Master
Mützchen, "the others are not properly there at all,
you must know. They are merely her thoughts, which
she spins around her over and over again. She has
been sitting there for a long time, and can't cross over
the threshold. Mutzeputz and I call it only the Gray
Lady's picture book, but neither of us likes to see it."

"It's not a pretty picture book," said Veronica.
"I don't understand why the gray aunt likes it so
much. Couldn't she be given another picture book?"

"Well, you see, Veronica," said Master Mütz-
chen, "in the picture book are the figures of those the
Gray Lady once lived with here in the house, on this
Earth, you understand, just as you are now on this
Earth. Now they are all dead, as it is called, and the
others went over the threshold long ago. Only she

could not, and now lives between two worlds with her picture book. It's an old tale; I am not supposed to tell it to you yet, Veronica."

"And I don't want to hear it. I think this picture book is horrible; I'm afraid of it, and I don't want to see it again."

"You must not go into the Green Room," said Master Mützchen. "You know already that Mutzeputz and I were not in favor of it. The picture book is only in the Green Room; that's probably the reason too why the mice moved out. They might have thought it was not the thing for their children. Of course the Gray Lady wanders all around here too, but that doesn't matter. You need not be afraid of her; she will always be very friendly with you. Now let's go and see your dolls. Surely they must be feeling lonely."

"Mutzeputz probably took care of them," said Veronica confidently. "He goes all over seeing that everything is in order."

"Yes, you can rely on Mutzeputz," said Master Mützchen.

This high opinion of Mutzeputz was justified. He was sitting among the dolls as Veronica and Master Mützchen stepped into the playroom.

"It's a good thing you've come at last," said Mutzeputz. "Peter and Zottel have been waiting a long time for you."

"Thank you for keeping an eye on my dolls," said Veronica.

Then she held out her hand to Peter.

"How do you do, Peter," she said.

Peter was older than Veronica, and really ought to have been going to school, but he was not able to. He was simple-minded, and it was infinitely hard for him to understand things. So he helped his father in the garden occasionally as well as he could, and played often with Veronica. Uncle Johannes took a great deal of trouble with him and tried to teach him a few things.

Now Zottel came up and offered his paw. Zottel was Peter's dog, a creature with a lot of long hair which hung over his face, so that most of the time you could only see one eye. Veronica often brushed and combed him and liked to part his hair. Zottel and Mutzeputz knew and esteemed each other. Intelligent and farsighted people rise above racial enmity. Mutzeputz and Zottel were a wonderful example of this.

"This is Master Mützchen," explained Veronica.

Zottel looked with one eye at Master Mützchen, and wagged his tail. Animals mostly see something of the other world. But Peter was not aware of Master Mützchen at all, and could not understand Veronica. He was just a little older, and no longer had the inner eyes that Veronica still possessed. It is possible he had never had them. He was so awkward in many things.

"Can't you see Master Mützchen?" asked Veronica.

Peter shook his head silently, and into his eyes crept the helpless look that he always had when he did not understand something. He closed his hand tenderly in Zottel's hair. The great love and devotion of the dog were some comfort and support for the poor boy.

Veronica was quite used to Peter's not seeing a good many things she talked about. So she gave a patient description.

"Master Mützchen is small and cute. I've been having a long talk with him. Look, he's as small as this," and she showed his size. "He has a red hat and little thin arms and legs, and he's absolutely darling."

Peter believed her. Peter believed everything Veronica said.

"You know, Peter," went on Veronica eagerly, so as to let her playmate take part in everything, "Master Mützchen showed me lots of thresholds and steps here in the house. You can fall over them if you don't watch out. You must pay attention, Peter, and take great care."

Peter promised.

"Master Mützchen was with me in the Green Room, where we've never been. There's a gray aunt there, who's nice. But she has a horrid picture book, and I don't want to see it ever again. Otherwise I'd show it to you, but you wouldn't really get anything out of it."

"Does the gray aunt live here all the time?" asked Peter.

New people were in some way a difficulty for Peter until he was familiar with them. Everything went very slowly with Peter.

"Yes, she lives here," said Veronica. "I hadn't seen her before either. She doesn't come to meals. Perhaps she doesn't eat anything; she looks so misty and altogether she is a bit funny. I can't explain it exactly."

Peter looked helpless. The thing was not clear to him.

"I believe it," he said.

"Perhaps Master Mützchen doesn't eat anything either," said Veronica, "and that's why he has such thin legs. All the same he looks nice. What a pity you can't see him. I wonder if my legs would get so thin too if I didn't eat any more?"

Peter did not know that. It was an entirely new problem for him.

"Now we'll play with the dolls," cried Veronica. "We'll all sit around the table, and Mutzeputz and Zottel must join us too."

"Thank you, no," said Mutzeputz. "I want some rest now and I will retire to the couch. I've been superintending your dolls all this time."

"That's true," agreed Veronica. "I am sure you are tired out."

Peter could no longer comprehend clearly what Mutzeputz said. But Veronica still understood quite well how to listen to thoughts and speak in thoughts. This was still left to her from the Garden of Spirits.

Peter and Zottel declared themselves ready to go along with everything Veronica suggested. Master Mützchen stood there and pulled monstrous faces. Veronica watched him fascinated.

"It's really too bad, Peter, that you can't see what marvelous faces Master Mützchen can make," she said. "It's simply wonderful. I don't know anyone who does it so well. But let's play at figures now. Master Mützchen can give us the problem, and we'll see who gets there first. For instance, if you take two from four. . . ."

Arithmetic was an abomination to Peter.

"I think that's very hard," he said.

"Didn't Uncle Johannes teach it to you?" asked Veronica. "Uncle Johannes is terribly good at it. He does it with nuts, you know. Then you can eat the nuts."

"He uses nuts with me too," said Peter. "Uncle Johannes is very patient with me, and he explains things over and over. He's sure I'll get it in the end. But I'd rather play something else."

"We could look at a picture book," suggested Veronica. "That's nice, and perhaps it's easier for you and Zottel than figures. Mutzeputz is tired, but I'm sure Master Mützchen will enjoy looking at the pictures."

Peter nodded with satisfaction. He agreed to everything as long as people did not ask him difficult questions. Master Mutzchen was obviously ready too, for he hopped onto the picture book in one bound, making Veronica laugh.

Then the Green Room came into her head again.

"Do you think the gray aunt is still looking at her picture book?" she asked curiously.

"We won't think about that picture book any more now, Veronica," said Master Mützchen.

*

But the Gray Lady's picture book was no longer alive in the Green Room. The thoughts of the Gray Lady had grown tired, and they no longer gave life to the remnants of the old bygone events. So her picture book had fallen to pieces, and the disintegrated forms had hidden themselves with all the other left-over things that hung around in every corner of the House of Shadows. They ought never to be called forth, but ever and again the Gray Lady awakened them in the longing and quest of her soul. Many are the dead who live in Houses of Shadows and cannot find their way over the threshold. They live in their picture book, and it often takes a long time until they understand this.

The Gray Lady sat sunk in her armchair, and her delicate pale hands played restlessly with costly antique rings—these too were nothing more than a reflection of herself.

Before her stood Johannes Wanderer. "Have you come back, Johannes?" asked the Gray Lady.

"Yes, I've come to help you. At least I'll try. Don't you think, Helga, that you could cross over the threshold? You've been far too long in the House of Shadows, and the way you are living you are not at home either here or over there."

"I feel this often, but all that is not clear enough to me," said the Gray Lady. "I can't do anything about it, and you can't help me either. You don't know all that has happened here, or at any rate you don't know it the way I do. I lived it, and I must live it over again. What should become of me otherwise?"

"That was so once, Helga, but it is no longer real. Try to understand that you are living with pictures, not people. There are left-over things in the House of Shadows, and you have enmeshed yourself in them."

"How do you know whether it was or whether it still is? I have just now been talking with all those who were sitting around me. I can't recollect anything else since the time I took poison here in the Green Room. I know that I fell asleep, and when I awakened everything was as it is today."

"It looks that way, Helga, because you can't cross over the threshold."

"Didn't Heinrich sit there a few minutes ago where you are standing now? Didn't his hand reach out to the sword as it did before, when he quarreled with his cousin?" asked the Gray Lady.

"Heinrich died a long time ago, Helga," said Johannes Wanderer gently.

"That's what they tell me, but how can it be? He was sitting there in front of me—or, isn't he still standing before me?"

The Gray Lady's beautiful eyes widened and stared in perplexity at Johannes Wanderer.

"Tell me, are you Heinrich or are you Johannes? I never know when I look at you. You are Heinrich and yet you are not."

"I was Heinrich and I am Johannes. I am not either of them altogether. These are only changed aspects of ourselves, Helga, those of us who set out on our wanderings."

"I can't quite understand this, but I speak to you as I used to speak to Heinrich. It seems as if I couldn't do anything else. You spoke of wandering. Is that why you are called Johannes Wanderer?"

"That is just a play on words, Helga, but every play hangs together a little with things. We all really have this name, because we all wander from one life to another, adding to ourselves and to the building of the world. The dead and the living are only different forms of one great existence. But you have stopped on the journey. No one should do that, Helga. You will understand me quite well, once you have crossed the threshold."

"That is difficult to grasp, Johannes."

"It's quite simple. It only looks difficult when we lose our way, and you have lost your way in the House of Shadows."

"Is it true after all that Heinrich is dead? It can't possibly be true," persisted the Gray Lady. "It was certainly foolish of me to believe it at the time. Oh, but there's no point asking you. You are Johannes Wanderer; what can you know about it?"

"I still know it very well, Helga. Look here, this is what happened. Heinrich and the other man both loved you, and so they quarreled. But you yourself didn't know which one you loved most. That was here in the Green Room, wasn't it?"

"Yes, it was here," said the Gray Lady, forlornly. "It was here at this table. Heinrich stood there, where you are standing now. It was only afterwards that I knew it was Heinrich that I loved most. But I was young and silly and vain, and I was flattered by the love of the other one. The next morning they fought out there on the heath, where the three birch trees are. The other one fell, and there was blood on Heinrich's sword. I couldn't get over it, and lay awake brooding night after night. Should I still love him or not? There was a dead man between us. Everything was horrible and confused. Heinrich had to flee abroad; it was very sad, but it was better for him."

"He went to Paris," said Johannes Wanderer. "Later on he didn't love you any more, Helga, not the way you think. He realized that it was only passion, one of the many digressions we make. How else could it have ended in blood? Love doesn't end that way. He fell in love with another girl, and knew that she was the companion of his soul."

"What was her name?" asked the Gray Lady excitedly.

"Is that important, Helga? What is a name? Ephemeral, like everything else. Only one name remains with us, which goes on from life to life. At that time she was called Madeleine de Michaille. It is of no consequence. I'm telling you all this only so that you may learn to forget Heinrich."

"Was she pretty, and was he happy with her?"

"I suppose she was pretty. But little Madeleine is long dead, Helga. He was happy with her and loved her very much, her and the gay life of Paris. But there was blood on his life, and you know why. Oh, Helga, all of us were foolish, as well as you. He paid for it. As the red hordes poured through the streets of Paris, he died on the scaffold, and she with him. Death wedded them."

A shudder ran through the Gray Lady, and her form shrank strangely into itself.

"That was the last I heard of him," she said, "and then I fell asleep here and woke up again so confused. Since then I can't recollect anything exactly any more. But they all come to me every day, and we talk about how it used to be. It is only about what you say of Paris that Heinrich can't tell me anything."

"Because you speak with his portrait, not with him," said Johannes Wanderer. "You must try to understand this, Helga. So much depends on it for you that you must grasp it in the end."

"I will make an effort," said the Gray Lady, "but where is Heinrich, if I am only speaking with his portrait?"

"He is on his travels. He went over the threshold into another world, and has come back again over the threshold to a new journey. All of us travel and seek, so that we may find. Only you, Helga, have stayed behind and have lost your way."

"If you too travel and seek, what have you found, Johannes?"

"I have found a great deal, but we must accept the fact that many things are still left to seek and to find. But we must travel and not stay behind."

The Gray Lady supported her head in her long narrow hands.

"You are not Heinrich," said she. "He did not speak the way you are speaking now. I have great confidence in you, Johannes, but I could not love you as I loved Heinrich."

"That is just as well, Helga. Between Heinrich and Johannes lies a long road. You shouldn't go back over it again."

"Whether you are Heinrich or Johannes, you are living now on this Earth and I, you tell me, between two worlds. I can well believe that, for the others don't see or hear me. How does it come about that you can see and hear me, Johannes—you and Little Veronica who was here today?"

"Veronica came back over the threshold not so long ago, Helga, and she still has the inner eyes which see beyond tangible things. As for myself, I have learned on my journeys how to awaken those eyes again."

"Is it very difficult, Johannes?"

"Yes, it is difficult. Only a few learn it, for it demands great sacrifices. But once you have learned it, you are across a great many steps and are able to help both people and animals. This is a wonderful task and of more value than what men call happiness. I want to help you, Helga, but you must want it yourself."

"I do want it," said the Gray Lady. "I have yearned for help for so long. But a miracle would have to happen for me to be able to cross the threshold, Johannes. It looks very big and very high to me."

"Miracles happen every day," said Johannes Wanderer.

"Possibly," said the Gray Lady, "but you see, when we lived together here—oh, I don't know now whether it was you or not—we didn't believe in miracles, Johannes. We scoffed at them! We laughed too about the church. Now, where I live between two worlds, I have often been in the church at Halmar, where I used to sit as a young girl. There were others there, too, who are like me and can't cross the threshold. But we have not experienced any miracle. The man who preaches now in Halmar church doesn't know what life and death are; he can't help us over the threshold. We all went away sadly, I to the House of Shadows and the others to the old corners and streets of Halmar, where they drift around and wait. No miracle has happened, Johannes. It is dark in Halmar church, not light. How gladly would we go back there if it were light. But how can we know?"

"You will hear about it all right when the light comes to it," said Johannes. "The dead learn of and know much that the living don't see yet. But it is true that there is no longer anything miraculous in Halmar church. But you must be patient, Helga, you and the others. We must all have a great deal of patience. Anyone who wants to be a priest must first experience a miracle in himself, before he can hold divine service. Wait until the pastor of Halmar becomes a priest. The miracle has always come to everyone who waited for it and called for it. Call for it every hour."

The Gray Lady smiled, at peace.

"I'll try," she said.

A faint golden glimmer wove its way into the darkness of the Green Room, and Johannes Wanderer gently closed the door behind him.

*

At supper Veronica was quiet and lost in her own thoughts. The day had tired her, and she hardly heard what her mother, Aunt Mariechen, and Uncle Johannes were saying. The three were sisters and brother. Aunt Mariechen had remained unmarried; she was the oldest, and was so completely wrapped up in taking care of everyone's needs that inwardly and outwardly she had become a picture of that activity. Nearly everyone called her Aunt Mariechen, even when she was not their aunt at all.

When Veronica had drunk her milk, she said suddenly, half to herself: "A gray aunt lives in the Green Room."

"The things you imagine, Veronica!" said her mother.

"There is a Gray Lady," said Caroline, who was removing the plates. She did not actually say it, she shouted it. Caroline shouted everything she had to say.

"How can you talk such nonsense!" scolded Aunt Mariechen, "and before the child, too."

"Because she really is there," shouted Caroline, and disappeared angrily with the dishes.

"You needn't be frightened of the Gray Lady, Veronica," said Uncle Johannes.

"Master Mützchen says so too, and I am not afraid," said Veronica.

"What's this now? Where does the child get these odd names?" said her mother. "Veronica, you can go out onto the porch for a little, if you've finished."

"Yes, Mama."

"Johannes," said Veronica's mother, when the child had gone out, "talk Veronica out of this instead of telling her that she needn't be afraid. Otherwise she'll end by thinking that the Gray Lady really exists. It's nothing more than idle talk, because it was in the Green Room that the tragic story of beautiful Helga took place. Her lover killed his rival in a duel, and it is said that she took poison. These are old tales, and already when we were children it was said that the Green Room was haunted, and a Gray Lady lived there. Children hear these tales from the servants, but one ought not to allow it."

"Dear Regina," said Johannes quietly, "one shouldn't tell a child an untruth. That's no good. It would be better if you told Veronica that she has nothing to fear."

"Do you really believe there's a Gray Lady there?" asked Aunt Mariechen, shocked.

"Certainly," said Johannes. "I know it for sure."

"I know you have your own views of many things," said Regina, "and I can't always follow you. It may be that there is more than we suppose. But where did Veronica get it from? Caroline must have told her."

"Probably Veronica saw the Gray Lady, Regina. Children often see more than adults. One must take that into consideration."

"We didn't see anything of it when we were children," objected Regina.

"Or we've forgotten," said Johannes. "We've forgotten so much, Regina."

"We were frightened because we were stupid," said Aunt Mariechen.

Johannes Wanderer was amused.

"Who knows whether we're so much cleverer today?"

"I certainly do," said Aunt Mariechen, annoyed.

"But, Johannes, you don't really think that Veronica . . ." Regina stopped, perplexed and uncertain. She was one of those people who never quite awaken to their own inner selves and so do not know which course to steer.

"That's all nonsense," said Aunt Mariechen clearly and vigorously. "You have had curious ideas, Johannes, since you came back from your long journey. You simply must eat more; then you won't have any more thoughts of this kind. You're undernourished, and the Gray Lady and all that nonsense doesn't exist!"

As Aunt Mariechen spoke, the Gray Lady was standing just beside her.

*

Veronica had sat down on the steps of the porch, and was looking at the garden. It seemed to have be-

come unfamiliar to her. Certainly it was a lovely garden, but hadn't it been different yesterday?

Veronica was sad; she did not know why.

It was the twilight which had come. The Garden
of Spirits had vanished; a veil had fallen between it
and Little Veronica. But the House of Shadows lived
around her and looked at her from a hundred mysterious eyes.

CHAPTER III

AARON MENDEL'S BURDEN

HE lonely northern country-side was once even more deserted than it is today. Only occasionally did a railroad track cut through the moors and heaths where stunted firs and little birch trees grew with difficulty, and no screaming motor-cars raised the dust of the endless highroads or disturbed the solemn stillness of the woodland paths whose green hedges were flecked with sunlight. How beautiful it was, this countryside, because it was sparsely populated, because—still far from a time of noise and confusion—it dreamed the innocent dream of its existence in the call of the animals and the breathing of the plants. The voices which spoke here were the voices of nature; the gently rustling treetops, the clear heaven above, sang always the same song, and the green moss carpet was embroidered into a miracle of the wilderness by the simple, gaily-colored flowers of the north. But the roads on which human life moved through these woods and heaths were little used, and one could journey far without meeting anyone.

It was at that time that strange figures trudged on pilgrimages over the lonely roads, traveling restlessly from farm to farm, from one small town to another. Old Jewish peddlers they were, each carrying a heavy bundle on his back. Untiring, their busy feet trod through the dust of the roads; humble and submissive, their shoulders bent under a far too heavy load. They wandered as Ahasuerus wandered, and the wind drove through their poor clothes and their gray fluttering hair. I still see them today before me, as I saw them when I was a child. Even today I feel something of my blissful expectation as they took the bundle from their back and showed the splendor of their wares. It was a whole chest they shouldered, made of wood and covered with a strong linen sack with straps. They would pull out one drawer after another, singing the praises of each, and dazzle one's astounded eyes with an abundance of infinitely alluring things. What treasures these walking chests contained! Decorative brushes and combs, ribbons in all colors and unimagined shades, pocketknives in overwhelming choice, printed neckerchiefs with improbable flower patterns, grass-green candies and chocolate rolls wrapped in colored shiny paper. Never again did one see a wrapping so mysteriously resplendent. Never again did one feel so much the bliss of purchase and also the limitations of possession. How carefully one had to figure and think things out, so as to secure one of these delights forever out of a tight pocket-money budget. How terribly hard every choice became, and how often it was complicated to the point of insolubility by the flood of words coming from these walking department-stores: "Never again will there be such an opportunity; combs, brushes like these are still to be had only this year, no, only today. After that you won't find them again all your life. Make no mistake! These pocketknives have been ground so sharp that they will cut a hair that falls on them!" You saw yourself already with cut and bleeding fingers. "These printed neckerchiefs, these ribbons—never again! The world will have to do without them; they are just too expensive to make. So this is the last time these patterns will be seen by a human eye. And this chocolate—no more! It's really crazy to sell it. And as to the prices—why, it's just giving them away." And now the last drawer is slowly opened like a curtain drawn back from a theatrical scene: jewelry and trinkets, coral pins, and rings in which cut stones made of glass sparkle in the sun. "Now, look at that. Where have you seen such brilliance? They are made of glass not only because of its low price, oh no! Above all it's because it is well known that glass is superior to all precious stones in light and color. You can't possibly get the same effect with the regular so-called precious stones. They would look ridiculous in comparison, wouldn't they? Anyone with even a little understanding of the matter must agree."

I still know today how exquisite is the joy of a

child in making such a purchase. Still better and more profoundly, however, I know how this feeling ended. I still see before me the old Jew closing drawer after drawer, then pulling the coarse linen sack back over the chest and hoisting it onto his shoulders with a jerk. At this moment suddenly the thought seized me: this pack is much too heavy for the old man, and he carries it along day by day, hour by hour, in rain, snow, and scorching sun over the endless highroad. What does he get out of his glorious things? They are not there for himself; he has to carry them around and he has to let them go. He even has to be glad if he gets rid of them, so that he may have bread to eat —bread which he may perhaps consume at the edge of a ditch or in a dirty inn on the heath where he sits in a corner while people laugh and poke fun at him.

Slowly, with the measured gait of long resignation, the old Jew disappeared along the highroad, and I watched him go, noticing how wearily he carried the pack along, how the straps cut into his shoulders, and the burden bent his back into a hoop. An infinite pity for the old man came over me, and the dearly bought fripperies burned in my hand like ill-gotten goods. In my soul, which had hitherto accepted everything with the ingenuousness of a child, the question formed itself: how would you like to wander like this? How would you like your father, your brother, to be in this old Jew's place, forced to carry this far too heavy load on tired feet across the highroads of an alien world? For the first time I understood something of the curse of man, and of the agony with which, alien and alone, he carries his burden through a darkened existence.

And a far-off foreboding whispered to me of countless heavy burdens one would see, and of the burdens one would some day have to carry oneself through life: loads against which you rebel, and which chafe you until you carry them with ever more quietness and resignation—before your eyes the goal that at the end of the journey you will set them down in a corner on the evening of the last day's toil, never again to take them on your shoulders. Human existence had opened its doors for a moment, and I had recognized its symbol in the poor old Jew on the dusty highroad carrying his far too heavy burden.

That was in the old days, and many years have gone by since then. Today another era has come to the lonely northern landscape, and the old Jews no longer wander from farm to farm. Life has changed and has found new forms of delight and many many more new forms of misery. But when Little Veronica lived in the House of Shadows the north country was still tranquil, and ever and again the wandering Jew was to be seen with his heavy bundle on his back, like a relic of bygone days that had come to a halt.

Such a relic was Aaron Mendel.

He was very tall and spare. But one did not notice how tall he really was, or know that he towered over most people when he straightened up. You did not see his true height because he stooped under his load, and because he had carried it around so many years that his shoulders had become bowed. Hair and beard were white, and hung unkempt and tousled, disheveled by the wind, and his face gave the impression that the weather in its manifold changes of spring, summer, autumn, and winter had graven on it innumerable signs and tokens. But his eyes gazed out strangely into the distance, as if he were searching for the unseen end of the road. Altogether he looked more like an apparition than a man from these parts. Superstitious people said of him that he had grown out of roots and the gray festoons of moss on the old fir trees, and, too, that he had no home, but wandered back from time to time into that wild forest over there to merge himself in it for a while and gather fresh strength from its soil. He might be much more than a hundred, perhaps even two hundred; no one knew exactly. Most people had known him when they were children, and they still bought from him although there were now stores in Halmar which carried the same things. But one bought for the sake of an old tradition, in the same way we enjoy walking today along a winding footpath where we walked as a child, rather than on new roads built by a new age.

Aaron Mendel did not need to go on praising his wares; that went without saying, as he himself did. And in an extraordinary way no one dared to beat him down in price, as was usual in other cases. Aaron Mendel had a dignity which by itself forbade this. There was something in him of the ancient grandeur of the Old Testament, which had strayed into a foreign land in an alien time, homeless, exiled, and condemned to wander, but had risen above the measure of all commonplace things like a ghost from the wilderness on Sinai. There were only a few people in the region stupid and arrogant enough not to feel it. However, Aaron Mendel seemed to overlook these.

Aaron Mendel seldom came to the farms around Halmar. He had aged considerably and traveled slowly and without his former energy. His visits looked more like a desire on his part too to keep up a tradition, rather than any particular concern about trade. He seemed to loom up out of this sort of tradition from time to time, as though conjured out of the ground, pacing tall and spare over the roads which his feet had trodden for so many years, with ever the same bundle on his back.

For years, too, it had been a tradition that he made a halt in Uncle Johannes' garden-house and had coffee with him. Aaron Mendel was for Johannes Wanderer a piece of his childhood; they had known each other when Johannes was a little boy going to school in Halmar. They called each other by their first names, without any formality, like old acquaintances who were pilgrims on the same road. Many a time that road is in this life, but far more often there are roads from former lives, which make it appear to people of the most different backgrounds and races as if they have already known each other a long time. The roads we travel have countless milestones, and many stand there rooted in a gray past and bearing an inscription which is hard to decipher. For all human beings, considered with the inner eye, are not only what they are today, or seem to be—their Today is only a small part of what they were and what they will become. Who is to know whether those whom we meet for the first time in this life are brothers and sisters, or companions of the temple from thousands of years ago? This may have been why Aaron Mendel, who was not talkative, talked a great deal when he was with Johannes Wanderer in the quiet garden house.

On one of these visits, Aaron Mendel, as usual, laboriously unloaded the heavy chest, untied the linen sack, and displayed the things in the drawers, which Johannes used to buy regularly. Chocolate for Veronica, Peter, and Zottel, many-colored ribbons for Veronica's dolls, a wool ball for Mutzeputz, who, in spite of his inner maturity, still liked to play with it, colored crayons for Peter, who could not write but loved to draw and paint in his clumsy way, and finally even a fantastic head scarf for Caroline. Caroline possessed a collection of fearsome scarves, and wore them like war trophies. The selection of these treasures Johannes Wanderer always left to Aaron Mendel alone, without making any choice himself—it was a question of tact and confidence, just as it would be with a very large firm one had dealt with for years.

When the usual purchase was taken care of, Aaron Mendel sat down on a high-backed chair and rested, while in a long, quiet interval Johannes prepared the coffee. With the coffee Aaron Mendel ate croissants and butter, another tradition. He was very fond of croissants, though he considered them a luxury not without sin, at least on an ordinary working

day. Aaron Mendel had his own thoughts about
everything, which he had laboriously worked out on
his wanderings. He had had time enough for them in
the dust of the highroad. Thoughts such as these are
the offspring of tranquility and loneliness, and one
should take more heed of them amidst the din of catch
phrases. They are not always correct, but they are always living things, born of a human soul, and on their
tracks life spins its invisible threads. For to live and
to understand life is to tread one's path on tired feet.

"Croissants are sinful," said Aaron Mendel as he
carefully spread a fresh croissant with butter. "Today
is not a holiday. And I've already had two cups of
coffee; it's against the just measure of things."

Johannes Wanderer poured Aaron Mendel a
third cup of coffee.

"You have taken on yourself quite enough of the
just measure of things already, Aaron. It doesn't do to
be too rigid. You are right to observe the appointed
holidays, but there are also holiday hours, which we
can create ourselves. And I count among these holiday
hours the moment when we sit together and the years
of old when I went to Halmar school come before my
eyes. Perhaps it is much longer than that that we have
known each other. One often feels oneself timeless.
Then it is that I think of an existence before this life.
Do you believe that there is nothing more to us than
that you have wandered the highroad year by year
and I have finished my schooling, traveled a little, and
now live in my lonely garden-house in order to pur-
sue my studies, help my sisters, and take care of

Little Veronica and the simple-minded Peter? I think this is not a sufficient explanation of the human in us."

"I've thought about that too," said Aaron Mendel, "but for me it's like a far country that I can't find. Many a time you dream yourself into it, but you are not really there."

"It is true that one is no longer there, but it is in oneself and from time to time it awakes and one remembers. When I see you before me like this, Aaron, I can well imagine you were once, a thousand years ago, a desert king bedecked with jewels and wearing a gold circlet in your hair. Couldn't it be that we once sat together as we are doing today? Perhaps we spoke of a future which is now the present. In ancient cultures men knew more about the metamorphosis of souls and about coming into being and passing away —more than they do now, when people have become loud-mouthed but are no longer so profound."

Aaron Mendel wagged his old head from side to side.

"Who can know that, Johannes? It could be, and it could well have been an easier life than today. We are outcasts, and we must accept it."

"That is true in a certain way," said Johannes Wanderer, "but we shouldn't wish the past back again. It is a mountain we must all strive to climb, and it is better to be Aaron Mendel halfway along the path than to remain below wearing a king's crown. No doubt the pull up is harder, but at the top all burdens fall away."

"And yet we have been outcasts since the Temple was destroyed," said Aaron Mendel.

"The Temple has been destroyed everywhere, not only among one race, Aaron. And we are all outcasts, but this is so that we may find light in the darkness and restore the Temple. If one didn't think so, how could one carry on? You must either accept this, or you must deaden your senses. Most people deaden their senses; that's why the times have gone astray."

"It is uphill work," sighed Aaron Mendel. "It's not only this pack I have been shouldering all these years. There was a lot more one hauled along, but one came to accept it."

"It is a great deal when one comes to accept things, Aaron, and for that reason you are greater today than before, when perhaps you were a king. I have always been very sorry that you have to carry this pack around, but you're right, it's not only this— it's also a symbol of all the burdens we carry. I have often wondered why this should be, for certainly many a burden is too heavy, as your pack is for an old man."

"I'm used to it," said Aaron Mendel simply.

"Yes, one gets used to it, but that cannot be the meaning of the burden. I've thought about it a lot, and it seems to me that the blessing of the burden lies in this, that men recognize one another as human beings and brothers. It's not only that—there are also hidden threads from former times which link us together, but I don't think, Aaron, that I would have come nearer to you if I had not been deeply affected by your trudging along the dusty roads carrying this burden. When we understand the burden, we no longer think, if we are human beings, about race, religion, and class, but only about people and about that which binds us together—the burden we carry. Isn't that the beginning of the rebuilding of the ruined Temple?"

"There are also people who don't see any burdens, and those who despise one for it," said Aaron Mendel bitterly.

"Those are the people who are still at the foot of the mountain. They live in a false glitter, and have not yet carried any burden. The nearer the summit our journey takes us, the more we know about the burden carried by human beings, animals, and plants, and in those who carry it we see our brother. I believe that it is for the sake of this perception that we do not surrender our burden. I won't say that I am glad to see you on the highroad, Aaron Mendel; God knows I'm not. I spoke only of the meaning of the burden, as I think of it. And I have nothing against the highroad; I know you can learn far more on it than in a comfortable life. But you're too old now. Is it necessary for you to go on dragging this heavy pack around? You'd do better to stay home in your little store, and if you think it should be expanded, I would be only too glad to help with it and find the money. None of us has much, but there's enough to allow for this."

"It's wonderful of you to say this, Johannes. I appreciate it very much, but my store is in no need of expansion. It is big enough, even when the day comes that I no longer go peddling on the highroad—we must call it by its right name, don't you agree? It's not bad—perhaps the contrary—for it is indeed a burden and that's the way I think of it. Certainly I could stay at home; my daughter Esther can easily look after the store by herself. She is a widow now, and only has little Rachel. It is a great joy to me that I have a granddaughter."

Aaron Mendel's weatherbeaten face glowed with a strange pride and bliss when he spoke of Rachel.

"Yes," said Johannes Wanderer, "but it seems to me that's just where you are far more needed. Little Rachel doesn't see much of you if you are away so much on your journeys. I don't travel or make trips any more now either, because I'm needed here."

"You are really needed where you are, Johannes. There is a tremendous amount of work to be done in the garden here, and though it's not a real estate any more since Regina's husband died, the two ladies wouldn't be able to carry on without you."

"That's the least important part of it," said Johannes Wanderer. "Regina and Mariechen have Peter's father, who is a very good gardener—at least in the garden. Unfortunately, he's not such a good gardener to his retarded child. The souls of children need even more careful handling than plants do. No, it's not for the sake of the garden that I must stay here. I am caring for another garden here, Aaron. Little Veronica and Peter need me. There are inner things which are stronger than the outer ones. There are threads

spun in the past before we were what we are today. I
must disentangle these threads, Aaron."

"I understand that," said Aaron Mendel. "There
are also inner things which are the cause of my wanderings."

"Won't you explain?"

Aaron Mendel drew his thin hand across his
forehead, and again that strange expression came into
his eyes, as if they were seeking in the distance the
invisible end of a road.

"It's a secret, Johannes, but I'll tell you. We've
known each other a long time, ever since you were
a schoolboy in Halmar, perhaps even longer in the
sense you meant it just now, but I find it easier to
dream of that than to comprehend it. It's a secret, and
I haven't told anyone else except Esther, because she
has to know why I can't stay home and why I have
to go on wandering. I know you won't laugh, because
you can see a bit behind things. It's not because I
have to earn money that I still trudge along carrying
this heavy pack. It is very heavy, and I can understand that you don't want me to go on with it. True,
I make a bit of money this way, for everyone still
buys from me out of long habit, Johannes, I know
that quite well, because they bought from me when
they were children, not because I have better mer-
chandise. But today it's hardly worth while, and it's
a terrible effort. And, too, the reason I go on wandering is not that I don't like to be with Esther and little
Rachel. How much, much more would I like to be
there! It's none of these things. Look, Johannes—"

Aaron Mendel's voice was hushed as if he walked on holy ground—"it's for Rachel's sake, and because the Temple is destroyed, that I must wander."

"You think you are building the Temple when you carry your burden?" asked Johannes Wanderer.

Aaron Mendel shook his head.

"The Temple is destroyed, Johannes. Who knows when it will be rebuilt? That's not what I mean. But there's a curse upon us: because of the destruction of the Temple we are outcasts and carry our burdens around through the dust of the road. Those who don't are deluded, for they don't atone for the ruined Temple, and the God of our Fathers will punish them. Surely it is possible for one person to carry another's burden, and when I bear my heavy pack along the roads I say to myself: 'You are doing this for Rachel; you are carrying the burden for her.' I'm too old, and God does not demand it of me any more for the sake of my atonement. I have been a whole lifetime trudging the roads, and I have helped to carry the curse of the outcasts. Now, when my heavy pack irks me on my way, it is for Rachel, and every step I make with my back bent under the burden lifts from Rachel something of the great curse. And I want to reconcile God toward her; I don't want her to travel a dusty road carrying the curse of the outcasts. Her shoulders must be free, her neck unbowed; her feet must tread the carpet of the meadows, and when the dark spirits of vengeance seek to lay hold of her, she must be able to laugh and say: 'Old Aaron Mendel has atoned

for me!' You see, Johannes, that is the secret of why I
continue to wander."

"These thoughts of yours are good and great,
Aaron Mendel, but I can't interpret the idea of atonement in such a gloomy way as you do. The old cultures have passed away; a turning point in time has
come; out of the curse a blessing must be created, and
out of the burden its true meaning. And Rachel too
must carry her burden like all the rest of us; you cannot take it from her entirely by a sacrifice. But the
strength of the love you put into your wanderings for
Rachel will help her to take upon herself the burden
of life. Love such as this is more than a sacrifice.
Goodness is the highest degree of strength a man can
attain, for it is of the substance of God."

"That is all true," said Aaron Mendel, "but I
can't think quite the way you do, Johannes. There
still remain vengeance, sacrifice, and the curse of the
outcasts. The ruined Temple must be atoned for. I
atone for Rachel when I make my journeys; I also
atone for Rachel when I mortify the flesh. You see,
Johannes, I know you always find it a bit peculiar
when I am so fussy about unimportant trifles, and when
I abstain from eating white bread on a working day.
It's not meanness or obstinacy when I deny myself
many things. It is for Rachel, for what I do without
she will have in abundance. I must go now, Johannes,
and must journey farther for little Rachel."

Johannes Wanderer grew sad.

"Do you want to travel forever, Aaron?"

"Until God takes the burden from me at the end of my days."

"Can it not be taken from you sooner?" asked Johannes Wanderer.

Aaron Mendel hoisted the heavy pack once more onto his shoulders.

"When the burden has grown so light that it is no longer a sacrifice," said he, "then I will give up traveling. That will be a sign from God. But do signs still appear, Johannes? It seems to me that it has become very dark everywhere, and no more signs speak to us."

"Signs still occur today, Aaron, and I hope and believe that God will not let you wander until the end of your days."

Johannes Wanderer escorted Aaron Mendel out. In the garden they met Veronica. Veronica gave Aaron Mendel her hand and dropped a little curtsy. She looked at him wide-eyed.

"You are carrying a heavy load," she said. "When I grow up I'll help you."

"Thank you very much for that, Veronica," said Aaron Mendel. "I shall not live to see you grow up, and I wouldn't let you carry my load anyway. It is too heavy for you. But today you have helped me carry it by saying that. I will remember it on my long road. Perhaps the signs are beginning to speak."

Aaron Mendel went through the garden gate out onto the highroad, and gave Johannes Wanderer and Veronica his hand in farewell. Tall and spare went his bowed figure into the distance in the light of the set-

ting sun. He had taken his hat off, and the wind ruf-
fled his white hair.

Johannes Wanderer and Veronica watched him a
long time.

"Uncle Johannes, is Aaron Mendel a king?"
asked Veronica. "Why does he wear a crown on his
head?"

"Do you see that?" said Johannes Wanderer.
"No, Aaron Mendel is not a king today. Perhaps he
was once. But he wears the crown you see because he
is carrying his burden for little Rachel. It is the king-
ship of the burden we carry for others."

"Do we have to do it, Uncle Johannes?"

"Everyone must do it of his own accord, Veronica. We must try to help one another with our burdens—human beings, animals, and every living thing.
That is the path toward the light."

CHAPTER IV

MARSEILLAISE

HE walls in the House of Shadows were thick and the windows narrow, so that the last rays of the sun faded early. The gray veil of dusk lay on Veronica's playroom and spread over everything in it, blurring the outlines, and making it look as though shadowy forms stood between those things which were clear and familiar by day. In the deep bay window sat Johannes Wanderer, reading by the last light trapped in it, and Veronica, sitting on the floor, was dressing up her dolls with the ribbons from Aaron Mendel's box. Mutzeputz lay beside her on a soft pillow, and Master Mützchen skipped around the room on his thin legs, making peculiar movements as if he were snatching at shadows.

"Uncle Johannes," asked Veronica, "you know who the Gray Lady is, don't you?"

"Yes, Veronica," said Johannes Wanderer, "but you mustn't think about her now. You can't help her."

"I would like to so much," said Veronica. "She

was very nice to me. Only I didn't like her picture book at all. Will she stay here a long time still and look at her picture book?"

"She is waiting until it grows light in Halmar church," said Johannes Wanderer.

"Is it dark there?" asked Veronica.

"It is not as light as it should be," said Johannes Wanderer. "But for the Gray Lady it must become light, otherwise she won't find her way over the threshold she has to cross. I know she could do it, and I have been at great pains to help her, but you see she only thinks now of Halmar church as it used to be long ago when she herself sat in it. So she waits for it to grow light, and in this lightness she believes she will find the way that will lead her into the other world."

"Can't the church be made light, Uncle Johannes?"

"*I* can't do it, Veronica, but it will certainly happen one day. People walk different paths, and the only thing that matters is that a light shines for them."

Veronica thought about this.

"Uncle Johannes, do you mean the three candles in the candlestick that the Angel showed me once?"

"Yes, Veronica, but each candle-flame has its own time and its own meaning. We must watch over them, so that one day the blue and red flames will merge with the golden flame burning in the middle. These are not easy questions, and this evening it would be much better if you played with your dolls and had a look at what Master Mutzchen is doing."

"You see Master Mützchen too, don't you? Oh, that's lovely of you, Uncle Johannes," cried Veronica enthusiastically. "I like him so much, and it's a shame that Mama, Aunt Mariechen, and Peter don't see him at all. They look at me so funnily when I talk about him. Only Peter believes in him."

"It is good for Peter that he believes so much," said Johannes Wanderer. "Then his three candles will burn as they should, even if he doesn't see them."

"I don't see the Angel and the three candles all the time either," said Veronica.

"That's not neccessary, Veronica. Your Angel keeps guard over them, and when you are older you will learn how to guard them yourself."

"Uncle Johannes, where is Master Mützchen sitting now? Can you tell that?"

Something like a shadow of doubt had arisen in Veronica's soul as to whether Uncle Johannes could really see everything, or whether he just said so as so many grownups do.

"Master Mützchen is crouching in front of the mirror, stretching his mouth so wide that it reaches from ear to ear," said Johannes Wanderer.

"Isn't that marvelous?" cried Veronica, full of admiration. "But you're really very clever, Uncle Johannes. Are you even cleverer than Mutzeputz? That I simply couldn't imagine!"

"I'd like to go on reading now," said Johannes Wanderer, "and as far as Mutzeputz and I are concerned, I wouldn't dare make comparisons. Besides, Mutzeputz is present and he can hear us."

"Mutzeputz is asleep; he has put his paws over his eyes," said Veronica. "When he lies that way, it means he's fast asleep."

"Who can be sure of that?" said Johannes Wanderer. "Anyway, Mutzeputz is very clever and a highly estimable person. I think he knows a lot that I don't know, and perhaps too I have learned things which may still be new to him. In saying this, I naturally don't want to set myself up above Mutzeputz; that would be very presumptuous of me."

"Uncle Johannes, Mutzeputz is purring. That means he heard what you said. But you are very clever too, and I am going to marry you now. Would you like that?"

"Very much," said Johannes Wanderer, "but I may go on reading while you do it, may I not?"

"Of course, Uncle Johannes; just sit where you are. I'll do it quite easily with the dolls. This doll is you, and the other is me, and now I'm going to marry us both."

Veronica put the dolls together and pondered.

"Wasn't it this way once?" she asked softly and a little perplexed, as if something had occurred to her that was unclear and that she could not quite grasp as yet.

"Don't do it with the dolls, Veronica," said Johannes Wanderer, looking up from his book. "Put two chairs for us there, but not the dolls. All kinds of shadows gather so easily near to dolls, fasten onto them, and grow much bigger than you meant them to be."

"Put the dolls away, Veronica," said Mutzeputz, tugging at her dress with his paw. "There's a blue light in the room, like there is for the Gray Lady's picture book."

"Oh, look!" cried Veronica, frightened. "The dolls look just like you and me now, Uncle Johannes, but now they're dressed in those queer clothes, like the Gray Lady and the others in the old pictures."

"Veronica, stop this!" said Johannes Wanderer, as he slammed his book shut and stood up.

It had become quite blue in the room, like moonlight weaving through rolling fog. In the blue light stood a black threshold, somber and strange. From far off there was the sound of drums, first soft, then swelling to a menacing roll.

"Don't go over the threshold, Veronica!" cried Master Mützchen.

But the threshold moved and advanced toward Veronica, and the dolls grew, stirred, and stretched their limbs.

And then there sounded, muffled as if through some thick material, but as near as if it were being sung in the next room by raucous voices:

"*Allons, enfants de la patrie . . . de la patrie . . .*"

Amid the tattoo of drums, the doors opened, and a figure in tattered uniform with a red cockade in his hat looked in and said something. He seemed to be calling out names, and through the receding roll of drums and the singing, Veronica heard clearly:

*"Citoyenne Madeleine Michaille! Citoyen Henri
. . . !"*

"No, I don't want to go; I don't want to!" sobbed
Veronica, hiding her face in her hands. "I don't want
them to take us away! Not yet, not yet!"

Johannes Wanderer caught Veronica in his arms
before she lost consciousness, and carried her to her
bedroom. Master Mützchen hurried in after them,
and Mutzeputz followed spitting, after knocking down
the dolls. But in the House of Shadows there was still
a sound as of a distant roll of drums and a slowly
fading singing of the Marseillaise: *"Allons, enfants
de la patrie . . . de la patrie. . . ."*

The playroom lay in darkness, and the dolls
moved no more.

*

When Veronica had been put to bed by her
mother and Aunt Mariechen, she came to from her
faint. But it was not a real awakening in this life.
The ghostly figure in the tattered uniform had disappeared, and she no longer heard the drum-beats and
the Marseillaise. She knew, too, that she was in her
own bed and that she was Little Veronica in the
House of Shadows. And yet she was not altogether
this. In an odd way she was freed from her body and
from everything that went with it.

All the things around her that were usually so
real seemed unreal to her, at least far less clear and
living than the pictures, which passed by her so quickly
that she could not have followed them with her usual

bodily eyes. But indeed she was not in the body; she was quite different from her usual self. She seemed to slide gradually out of her body and now stood beside it, so that she saw it lying in front of her like an image which resembled her but yet was now no more meaningful than a cloak. It was no longer her real self. No, that could not be herself; perhaps it was one of her dresses—that was how it looked, more or less. She felt herself outside it, standing by her bed, but without her feet having touched the floor. It was as if she were floating, and she was no longer a child, it seemed; she was much older and taller, and every-thing that surrounded her in her present childhood existence affected her hardly more than a dream only dimly remembered.

More real, much much more real, were the brightly colored pictures which unrolled themselves before her on an unending canvas, one woven into the other as if they were all there almost at the same time. And now she herself slipped into these pictures as one of their living figures, and was carried along by the current of their events. All these happenings, however, were known to her; it was as if she relived, backward, a life that she had once lived. Only it went so terribly fast that there was hardly any more real time which you could hold onto.

Yes, she knew it all. There were the streets of Paris, but they lay quiet and sunny; there was no horror in them yet, no blood and no shouting of sin-ister people with red cockades. She was wearing a silk dress, and by her side walked a cavalier with tri-

corn and sword—strange, how he reminded her of
Uncle Johannes. That high doorway over there with
the figures of saints was Notre Dame; she saw the
half-light of the church and the perpetual lamp inside,
and she crossed herself. "*Sainte Marie, concue sans
péché, priez pour nous. . . .*" Oh, how many pictures
glided past, ever new ones, and she was always in the
middle of them. Now she grew smaller and smaller;
she was a child again and was sitting in an old park
under blossoming trees. Wasn't this Madeleine in the
place where she had grown up? Near her in the sunshine lay a large cat. Could that be Mutzeputz?
Though Mutzeputz didn't have black markings like
these on his back.

But then the picture changed. Madeleine's park
became a Garden of Spirits. Oh, when had she last
been there? Wasn't there a Beetle who wanted to
show her his country-house, an Elf in the tree, and a
Sylph with butterfly wings who led her to the Silver
Bridge? Yes, that was it, and now the Silver Bridge
was there again, and now she saw the water across
which the bridge was built. Crystal clear it was, and
it moved unceasingly, alive in itself, but without
waves. She plunged deep into it and bathed. Pure delicate pearls were its substance, and it penetrated you
completely so that you bathed inwardly with your
whole being, and it was as though everything in you
became new and young like a primal morning you
saw and lived in. Everything was new; it was first
youth, and the pictures through which you had glided
were forgotten too.

But it did not last long. The water disappeared again; new pictures unfolded before Veronica's eyes, and she slipped again into their current with the same speed.

This was Holland with its windmills. In dark, narrow streets high-gabled houses huddled close together, their colored tiles reflected in the muddy canals of Amsterdam. There Rembrandt painted, here Spinoza lived. She knew these names for sure—or didn't she know them any more? The fat woman over there standing over her shining saucepans, wasn't that Aunt Mariechen? How terribly fast everything went! Now she was standing in a brocade gown, with a mask on her face; around her were nothing but gaily colored figures in a glittering ballroom. Laughter, lights, and music—this was the Carnival of Florence! Again Johannes Wanderer was beside her, silently pointing to a door. But she laughed at him and threw him a rose. Then the door opened, and the Plague entered, in a jester's tinkling costume, a grin on its death's head. Shrilly the violins broke off, the candles went out, and in the ugly gray of early morning corpses in festive array lay on the flagstones, glassy eyes staring out of the holes of the masks. Outside the bells tolled the Miserere. What a relief it was, after this horrible picture, to plunge into the crystal water, which ever and again pushed its way afresh between the spate of happenings, and cleansed you with its cool pearls! Now it was a Greek temple, in which Veronica stood tending the fire that burned in the copper brazier. Before her knelt a woman at the altar—wasn't it her mother? Now the Egyptian desert appeared, and bronze-colored people were working busily in the scorching sun to build huge pyramids. Again Veronica was in the midst of it, but this time she was oddly changed, and it seemed to her as if she were a man, wearing a sword-belt and sword and a headdress with the emblem of the royal serpent. Beside her she saw slow-witted Peter. He held a stone tablet in his hand, and was deciphering secret hieroglyphs—how extraordinary, since today he could neither read nor write! She had no time to think this over; everything scurried past so quickly.

Then the clear water closed over her for longer than usual, and when she came up out of it she was in a lonely country with snow mountains in the distance and with a splendor of flowers in glowing colors in the depths of the valleys. Enormous elephants shuffled past her on their column-like legs, nodding their heavy heads. From a temple, its roof a welter of carved stone tendrils, sacred monkeys chattered, stretching out their comical long arms to beg for fruit. But in the inmost depth of the temple it was quiet, absolutely quiet, and now Veronica sat there, naked but for a loincloth of plant fibers, as a young girl before an old man who was teaching her the secrets of existence. Oh yes, that was Uncle Johannes, and everything came back to her that he had once told her about the chain of things, about the ruined Temple of God, and about the wandering of human souls over dusty roads, in humility and devotion, and in service to every living thing. How profound was this stillness in the temple, how white were the distant snow mountains, and how clearly burned the three flames in the candlestick that stood before her. Three lights there were—blue, red, and gold.

The snow mountains, the valleys, and the temple vanished, but the lights remained. It was only these candles that Veronica still saw, and her Angel who held them up high in front of her. She recognized him. It was her Angel, and these flames lighted her existence. They were once more the three candles of Little Veronica, and she slipped slowly back into her body, and again was in her bed in the House of Shadows.

The Angel held his hand over the blue flame.

It burned the strongest of all. But now it flickered and grew smaller and smaller. The Angel watched over it, and now it leaned toward the golden light in the middle.

Veronica smiled peacefully, as children smile, for now she was a child again. She looked around the room and recognized everything. This was ordinary reality again, and all the colored pictures seemed to her like a far-off dream which grew ever fainter, like the blue flame in the candlestick which the Angel held.

She saw her mother, Aunt Mariechen, and Uncle Johannes sitting by her bed. Mutzeputz and Master Mützchen were skipping around on the floor. Mutzeputz was on his hind legs, holding Master Mützchen's hands with his front paws, and they were dancing together. Veronica couldn't help laughing.

"Thank God," said her mother, "the fever has gone."

"Now we can relax," said Mutzeputz. "Little Veronica is laughing again. You see what a good idea it was for us to dance? It cheered her up. How could anyone help feeling cheerful when we two dance together?"

Then he sprang purring onto Veronica's bed.

"You're well again now, Veronica, aren't you?" asked Aunt Mariechen. "We were very worried about you."

"Veronica wasn't sick," said Johannes Wanderer, "but it often happens that one flame burns brighter than the others."

Then the Angel covered the candlestick with the three candles, and Veronica fell asleep.

*

The next morning Dr. Gallus came over to Halmar to see Veronica. Her mother had sent for him, as she wanted to be sure that yesterday's fever was nothing serious.

Dr. Gallus was small and very agile. His close-cropped gray head darted from side to side, and this movement, together with a big nose and thick round spectacles, gave him the look of a bird. Added to all this, he spoke in curious snatches, as if he were snapping a beak at something and hurriedly swallowing all fears and objections anyone expressed. Now and then his tongue was rather sharp, but the people of Halmar were very fond of him because he never shirked any troublesome duty in his profession. Most of them likened him to the old parrot which lived with him, and many people called him by that name.

Dr. Gallus examined Veronica thoroughly, but he could not find anything that might have been serious. Master Mützchen stood behind him and aped everything he did. Veronica had to swallow hard to keep from laughing.

"You are pretty cheerful," said Dr. Gallus. "Next time you can come along to me and meet my parrot."

Then he snapped his mouth shut and pushed her gently out of the door.

"It's nothing new," he told Regina. "Veronica is very delicate, as I've always told you, and you must be very careful with her. And she shouldn't go to school in Halmar—we've already talked this over. She can have lessons here in the house. But there's nothing the matter, no, nothing. Hrrr-mph!"

"But she fainted yesterday," Regina objected, "and afterwards she undoubtedly had a fever. She spoke French, and it was uncanny how well she spoke. She hasn't learned that much French yet. And later on she babbled about foreign countries, elephants, and monkeys."

"This is a passing weakness," said Dr. Gallus. "There's no evidence of sickness, ma'am."

"But the French, the elephants, and monkeys?" said Aunt Mariechen. "You don't think that's dangerous, doctor?"

Dr. Gallus snapped at Aunt Mariechen.

"Absolutely not, as I said. I only wish I could have a fever which allowed me to speak better French, and as to elephants and monkeys, I'd like to see them too. There are none of these things in Halmar, are there? Hrrr-mph!"

"It seemed terrible to us. Where should the child learn anything at all about elephants and monkeys, just for the very reason that there aren't any here?" complained Aunt Mariechen.

"Good heavens, she's not a baby," said Dr. Gallus, "and there are enough picture books here in the house, with this sort of thing in them, aren't there?"

"The good French was really extraordinary," said Regina; "that struck me too. The rest is more easily explained, though I can't remember whether there are actually any monkeys and elephants in Veronica's picture books. There could be."

"Yes, ma'am, dreams often bring increased powers," said Dr. Gallus, wagging his head from side to side. "If we tried to get to the bottom of all this we would soon become monkeys and elephants ourselves, and who knows what else. My parrot too says all sorts of things I don't understand."

"I'm afraid Veronica is undernourished," said Aunt Mariechen.

Dr. Gallus knew Aunt Mariechen and her craze for nutrition, and snapped at her hastily like a bird at an insect.

"Dreams come more easily from a full stomach than an empty one," said he coldly. "Veronica is very delicate, but that's her whole constitution. She is well nourished. Don't stuff her under any circumstances."

"Veronica doesn't eat meat, doctor," complained

Aunt Mariechen agitatedly. "She doesn't like it, she says. Just like Johannes since he came back from his journeys saying so many peculiar things."

"It is not necessary for Veronica to eat meat," said Dr. Gallus. "She should eat whatever she fancies. Human beings and monkeys are close relations, and monkeys are vegetarians too."

Aunt Mariechen shuddered.

"But Veronica isn't a monkey!" she said, shocked.

Dr. Gallus' laugh held a touch of asperity. He liked to bait Aunt Mariechen a little.

"Well," said he magnanimously, "Little Veronica is not a real monkey, it's true, but we all resemble them."

Aunt Mariechen held up her hands defensively.

"I'm not a monkey," she said with the deepest conviction.

"Monkeys are clever animals," snapped Dr. Gallus dryly. "Anyway, they live more reasonably than we do. We really ought to take a leaf out of their book. Good morning, ladies, and for the time being you have no need whatever to worry."

Regina thanked Dr. Gallus and went with him to the door. Aunt Mariechen was speechless. But then the thought came to her: perhaps Johannes had lived among monkeys during the whole of his trip, and that was why he had grown so peculiar?

"All that about the monkeys can't refer to us, Regina? Not to Veronica, or you, or even to me? That would be unthinkable," she said, concerned.

*

Veronica had gone down to Johannes Wanderer in the garden, and the two of them were looking at the flowerbeds.

"Uncle Doctor is quite pleased, and I am to go and see his parrot," said Veronica. "But, you know, it was really funny yesterday. At first the man was horrid, but afterwards it was absolutely lovely, and I felt as if I were somewhere else where I had lived before, and everything went so fast, much faster than things go here. Tell me, Uncle Johannes, was it something like the Gray Lady's picture book? I can't explain properly. Everything was real; you must believe that. Aunt Mariechen thinks that it is only because I eat too little, and Mama says that I was only dreaming because I had a fever."

"It was quite real, Veronica," said Johannes Wanderer; "you can say too that it was a picture book, but different and much more alive than the Gray Lady's picture book. In former times you lived the way you lived backward yesterday; you'll understand it more fully later on. You see, it's just like the flowers which bloom today and die tomorrow, and then later they come out of the earth again and bloom once more."

"You were in the picture book too, Uncle Johannes, and I can remember that it was in a temple, and as well as you there were some adorable monkeys."

"That's very nice, Veronica," said Johannes Wanderer. "Monkeys are pleasant people, and in ancient India they were sacred animals."

"You know," said Veronica, "I would have remembered much, much more, but clear water always came in between and washed everything away; and that was lovely, too."

"We must be very thankful for that, Veronica. Without the crystal water which cleanses us, we couldn't bear all that painful trudging along the dusty roads of life. The clear water takes from us the burden we carry and makes us young again, just as if it were early morning."

"Yes, that's just the kind of feeling it is," said Veronica thoughtfully, "but if these are burdens that we carried, do we have to keep them and carry them further, or should we forget them?"

"We certainly must carry many of them further, until they fall from us completely, but we shouldn't always think about them," said Johannes Wanderer. "We have to start life new again, just as the flowers bloom anew, but each blossom must be more advanced than the one before. From time to time we must remember our old burden, when the blue flame burns in the Angel's candlestick. The weight of the burden we may forget, but we must guard its meaning within ourselves."

"And what about Mutzeputz and Master Mützchen? Is it the same for them?"

"Their way is a little different from ours, Veronica, but in many things it is the same for them as for us. All of us change and grow into the light; we are all brothers and sisters and flowers in the Garden of God."

CHAPTER V

IRRELOH

N old building is like an old
story hewn in stone, decorated with strange devices
and signs like a carefully illuminated chronicle. Such an
old chronicle was Castle Irreloh, and its walls spoke a
sinister language to those who could read it. Castle
Irreloh was much farther from Halmar than was the
House of Shadows. A dark fir-wood surrounded it
and rose gradually, spreading into the pine-covered
dunes. Behind them lay the sea. The green waves of
the Baltic rolled in white-crested, and beat monoto-
nously on the sand and on the tarred black fishing
boats tied up here and there along the shore. And the
song of the surf carried as far as the quiet park of
Irreloh. On the other side of the castle the red heath
stretched out, and the path to the House of Shadows
led across this and on to Halmar with its narrow
winding streets and little old houses dominated by a
church spire. The sound of the surf did not carry so
far, and that was as well, for the surf had nothing to
say to the peaceful houses of Halmar, but it had much

to tell Castle Irreloh, and told it day and night. The surf sang old and sad tales, and it would have been well for Castle Irreloh if it no longer had to listen to them. But it had to hear them because they were tales which were also part of the old chronicle of Irreloh. They whispered in the old walls the same song that the surf sang, and they spoke their own sinister language to everyone who could hear and understand. Not many people alive now could do so, but the letters and signs of the old tales are everywhere, even if they are no longer read or understood.

Would it not be better if one could still read the washed-out letters and decipher the intricate signs? Would men not see more clearly where the paths and byways they are treading lead, if they paid more attention to the ground on which they set foot? You who walk the Earth today, consider how many have trodden these ways before you, loved and hated, prayed and sinned. The sand of the shore you walk on has already received so many footprints and seen so many blown away—in sorrow and joy your speech is mixed with far, strange voices, in your thoughts other thoughts that once were thought here, and in the wreaths that you weave out of life invisible hands bind faded flowers that once blossomed in bygone days. All events are so strangely interwoven. How much could be made clear, how much avoided, if we could go through this existence with greater awareness. But we wander through the deep twilight that has come over us, and the shadows of olden times go with us.

Would you have come to Castle Irreloh, Ulla
Uhlberg, if you had understood the song of the surf,
if you could have read the writing on the old walls,
and the signs on the dark archway? Would you have
come if you could have seen how many withered
wreaths hung in the corridors and halls, and if you
could have heard how dead voices told each other the
story of Irreloh? Of course you came here to be near
the one you love. But Castle Irreloh is no place to prepare a bed of roses. Its gray vaults choke the bliss of
secret love dreams, and cold ghosts snatch at your
longing thoughts. Strong and proud you may be,
Ulla Uhlberg, but you will not be strong enough to
banish the ghosts of Irreloh. Besides, you know nothing about them. How can you fight and conquer when
you do not know what it is you have to fight and
conquer?

No, Ulla Uhlberg knew nothing of the ghosts of
Irreloh. As a little girl she had gone to school in Halmar after the early death of her parents, when she
came to live with an aunt there. It was a quiet world
in which the children of Halmar grew up, and the
little town and its narrow streets became her home.
But Ulla Uhlberg longed for the great, the boundless;
she dreamed of pomp and splendor, of life and laughter in glittering halls, and when she dreamed of such
things it always seemed to her as though she knew it
all, as though she had come from such places and
must return to them. But she knew little of the world,
and Castle Irreloh with its unwieldy mass always
seemed to her an alluring contrast to the peace of

Halmar, which, though quiet and restful, was always a little confined and boring. When Ulla Uhlberg grew up she inherited the large fortune of her parents. First she went traveling. She was young and rich, and had time to see the world. But she did not stay abroad. She returned and bought Castle Irreloh, for many years deserted, empty, and somewhat dilapidated. Ulla Uhlberg had now certainly seen enough of the world to realize that Irreloh did not represent pomp and splendor. No indeed, it was certainly not one of the noble houses of Florence that she loved so much. But she had spun her childhood dreams around Irreloh, had drawn invisible threads around its old walls, and it seemed to her that it must be here that she would experience the miracle that she had longed for in the seclusion of her early youth. She wanted to feel power and to rule, but she wanted it here; here in this place. She wanted to be great where she had been so small. Or was it perhaps her home that called her back again? It is so hard to say how many and incalculable are the various sensations that arise in the human soul—a man often does not know himself; he only hears one voice and does not dream that there are many voices. He desires something, but can never say exactly why he desires it. Ulla Uhlberg had no really strong home ties. She was not a pure Northerner like the others who had grown up with her in Halmar. Even as a schoolgirl she had been different, with her black hair, brown eyes and the unusual brown tone of her skin. No, she had felt more at home in Florence, under the deep blue sky and the radiant colors of the South, than she did here where snow and gray mist were more frequent than sun and clear skies. And yet she came home and bought Irreloh. It was not only the castle of her childhood dreams that she wanted to possess, it was that she wanted to be near all that she had dreamed into it, and that was so much. We none of us know where we are really at home; and how seldom we succeed in straightening out the tangled web of our life before death takes it out of our hands and a new design is woven from it on the loom of eternal creation!

No, today Ulla Uhlberg was not a little schoolgirl any longer; she recognized real beauty and splendor, and she saw quite clearly how dark and gloomy Castle Irreloh was. But it was not for nothing that she was so beautiful and young and strong, and she had built as much on the old walls of Irreloh as she once did in her childhood dreams. And when the surf sang far off, when the oak doors creaked, the thresholds groaned, or her step echoed in the deserted corridors, she laughed with the confidence of youth and without a care. She was mistress of Irreloh, and she meant to transform it and breathe into it the warm magic glow of the South that lived in her own soul. She would surround these gray walls with red roses, and one day her kisses would waken to life the dream of her childhood.

You are young and beautiful and strong, Ulla Uhlberg. But will you be strong enough to banish the ghosts of Irreloh? Life is so different from our dreams. We wreathe flowers and forge chains for ourselves.

With everything that is in us we summon to ourselves powers, both good and evil. Within yourself you tend a fire that is red and smoldering. In Irreloh too they tend old fires that once burned there. But the fires of Irreloh were false fires. You must remember that. Fire attracts fire, and none of us knows just how much remains only a symbol behind reality, and how much will come to birth some day of destiny out of a mysterious castle.

*

Ulla Uhlberg was sitting in a high-backed chair in the hall of Irreloh. The doors into the garden stood open and the golden light of summer was dancing on the heavy dark Renaissance furniture, which formed a suitable frame for Ulla Uhlberg's somewhat austere beauty. Pastor Harald Haller from Halmar and his wife were sitting opposite Ulla. They had been invited to luncheon and were now having coffee in the hall. Johannes Wanderer had just come in, and was sitting a little apart from the others in a deep bay window watching Pastor Haller, who was talking eagerly and explaining his liberal theological views. He had been doing this during the meal, and Ulla Uhlberg had to force herself to take a polite interest. It was a matter of the utmost indifference to her whether Pastor Haller was liberal or orthodox, and she only longed passionately for him to go so that she could be alone with Johannes Wanderer. Her fingers played restlessly with a fine gold chain of Venetian work around her neck. The butler served silently.

Pastor Haller was a man of good appearance, tall and still fairly young, with a serious, intelligent face that reminded one more of a professor than a clergyman. His wife was pretty in a superficial way, amiable and a little shy.

"Naturally it is not easy to introduce modern ideas into Halmar," said Pastor Haller. "The people here are backward; they believe in all sorts of miracles, even in ghosts, in 'gray ladies,' and 'little men.' It is hard to break them of this and to lead them into the present day and the spirit of enlightenment. Again and again I have to assure them that in Jesus it is only the moral example that matters, not the old Christian legends, however poetic."

"I am sorry that you can't get to feel at home with the people here," said Ulla Uhlberg politely.

If Pastor Haller only knew how utterly indifferent she was! But she smilingly offered him another cup of coffee.

"I can't say that I don't feel at home here; no, I feel very comfortable here. But, you see, the people don't live in the present day; they live in a past that can't face up to modern existence and the discoveries of today. I find that unwholesome, and I am trying in every way to change the outlook of these people. One can't remain stuck in the Middle Ages forever.

"But Harald dear," broke in Mrs. Haller shyly, "Father was a clergyman like you, and he always held firmly to the Bible and said one should not leave any of it out. Father was very much loved by his congregation, and I can't help feeling as he did. The people here would surely like you better if you left them all their miracles."

"Yes, dear child," said Pastor Haller thoughtfully, "your father's views were the opposite of mine; but of course the times were different. I don't want to criticize him. But we must take the present into consideration; the completely altered way of life, modern science, technical achievements, all these things are factors that we cannot overlook. People don't believe any more in miracles in the old sense; the legends are beautiful parables, but what matters is to have a human example in Christianity. The superstition of past times can no longer be reconciled with our modern knowledge."

Mrs. Haller fell silent and looked unhappy. She felt vaguely that in the proud academic structure of her husband's views there was something that did not quite fit, and she sensed in her simplicity much more clearly than he did that the people of Halmar had a strong aversion to this new teaching in church. It seemed, too, like some sort of menace to her own home.

Ulla Uhlberg suppressed a yawn.

Pastor Haller became unsure of himself and looked for some support.

"Mr. Wanderer," he said, "you are always so obstinately silent. Now I come to think of it, I have very seldom heard you speak. What is your opinion on these matters? You too have surely occupied yourself with religious questions from time to time."

"I think that a life without miracles is very poor," said Johannes Wanderer. "I wouldn't like to live one.

I also see in Jesus of Nazareth more than just a great man whose example should be lived up to. And for the most part, anyway, neither the liberal nor the orthodox does succeed in living up to him. There may be people who can live with a moral doctrine, but it seems to me not enough to die with. Yet living and dying are both close to us every day."

Pastor Haller cleared his throat. This quiet man, always aloof in company, now gave him an uneasy feeling.

"Well, yes," he said, "certainly this moral doctrine has to be set forth and translated into deeds, but surely we cannot expect the enlightened intelligence of today to accept miracles any more."

"I certainly don't uphold orthodox intolerance, or any other kind either, but to me a religion without miracles is no religion. Miracles still occur today; every flower is one, and modern natural science cannot explain the miracle of life and death."

"After all, we have come closer to many things," returned Pastor Haller.

"Or gone very far from them. Intellect and spirit are not the same thing."

"In the end it is you who will be preaching the Word to the people of Halmar, and be nearer to their ghosts than to me?" asked Pastor Haller jokingly, but there was a little sharpness in his tone, though he meant it to sound harmless.

"Frankly, yes, Pastor," replied Johannes Wanderer calmly.

Ulla Uhlberg smiled in amusement.

"But whatever kind of views are these?" asked Pastor Haller, shocked. "What is your direction in religious matters?"

"No particular direction," explained Johannes Wanderer pleasantly. "I don't think much of so-called directions. But I do think that a person, and especially a priest, can take only one road, and that is the Road to Damascus, and how that happens in each individual case doesn't seem to me to matter much."

Pastor Haller stood up. Really, this strange man was not much more advanced than the simple people of Halmar. That is what comes of traveling in the Orient.

"Well, yes, it depends how one looks at it, certainly," he said, avoiding the issue. "But now I am afraid we must be going, dear lady. Thank you so much for your kind hospitality."

"I am sorry you can't spare any more time," said Ulla Uhlberg politely. "The carriage is ready."

"It is very kind of you to have thought of that, but we could quite well have walked home," said Mrs. Haller.

"It is a long way to Halmar," said Ulla Uhlberg, "and of course I thought of it when you said you would have to be leaving soon after luncheon."

Ulla Uhlberg accompanied her guests to the carriage. Then she came back to the hall and seated herself near Johannes Wanderer.

"Now at last I have you to myself for a little while," she said with relief. "Pastor Haller means well

with all his modern enlightenment, but to me it is
dreadfully boring and completely irrelevant."

Johannes Wanderer laughed.

"To you, perhaps," he said, "but not to the people of Halmar. They want to find something in church
that they can hold onto, and they are right. The altar
is not a professor's chair for theological research, and
in spite of all our modern knowledge it is very dark
in the church at Halmar, as someone once remarked
to me."

"Who said that?" demanded Ulla Uhlberg. "It is
interesting that anyone should see it and express it in
this way."

"I can't explain, Ulla; the person who told me
that is between two worlds."

"How mysterious that sounds," said Ulla Uhlberg. "But tell me rather something about yourself,
Johannes. You haven't been to see me for a long time.
In our schooldays in Halmar we were together every
day. Aren't you burying yourself rather too much in
your studies? How are Regina and Mariechen, and
what is Veronica doing?"

"Thank you, Ulla, they are all well at present.
Veronica had a little fever, but it wasn't anything
serious. Regina and Mariechen have plenty to do, and
the market-garden is coming along nicely. It makes a
welcome addition to their income. I help them wherever I can. Gardening is so worth-while. It is a liveli-
hood and beauty combined, even though much of it
is pretty wearisome."

"Has Regina really gotten over the death of her husband?"

"I think so. It was a good while ago, and I never had the impression that they were very close to each other. As a general rule marriage is hardly more than a habit. And anyway, Regina seems to me a person who has never fully awakened. She never says definitely yes or no to any of life's questions. I have often tried to pin her down, but she always seems in rather a muddle even where Veronica is concerned."

"It was sad for Veronica to lose her father so early," said Ulla Uhlberg thoughtfully.

She was thinking of the early death of her own parents. Johannes felt that.

"She still has her mother, so it is rather different from your case, Ulla. And she has her home. I can't believe that Veronica would have had much from her father. He was so completely different from her. I recognize of course the ties of blood, but one should make no mistake that they come second. The spiritual relationship is stronger. One seldom finds both together. I mean that Veronica's nature is closely bound to Regina, but only a little to her father. It was Regina who had to work out her destiny with him, not the child."

Do you believe that or do you know it, Johannes?"

"In this case I know it," said Johannes Wanderer. "When Veronica comes to die, her father won't be the first to meet her. There are souls nearer to her on the other side as well as here. He is traveling a

path quite different from Veronica's, and at present it
seems to me that his way won't be a very easy one.
He was too far from the spiritual world, and it will be
a long time before he finds his way to it."

"Did you see that, Johannes? Can one see the
dead as well as the living?"

"Yes, one can, Ulla. The dead and the living work
more closely together than people believe, and together
they are building this world and the other. Today,
however, since we have become more material and
earthbound, the separation from the dead seems to us
unbridgeable. The ancient cultures thought and felt
otherwise. I don't want to pretend that I know about
these things, but, you see, there are some things
which I did learn on my travels. These travels were
'wanderings'—in the sense of voyages of discovery.
You will understand, Ulla, what I mean by that."

Ulla Uhlberg considered this.

"I haven't traveled in this way. I can't say that I
'wandered,' unfortunately. But I was in Italy, and you
in Asia. I can imagine that one learns a lot there, and
looks at some things differently from the way one
does here."

"Oh, that would be the least of it," returned Johannes, "and besides, I was helped. We have to help
each other, Ulla. Life is very hard if you come to
think it over and try to find your way in it."

"Does the simple life here satisfy you?"

"Yes, Ulla, I am hoping to be able to make it a
full life."

"Tell me, Johannes, did you come back because

of Veronica, or to help your sisters, or—perhaps for
some other reason? You broke off your travels very
suddenly."

"Of course I felt called upon to help Regina
when her husband died, but it is true that the call was
really to help Veronica. Mariechen doesn't need anyone; she is quite self-sufficient in her housekeeping."

"You were called?" asked Ulla Uhlberg.

"Yes, Ulla, not outwardly but inwardly. I am
very close to Veronica and must help her; these are
the laws of another world. I have to help Peter too."

"That is very beautiful, Johannes, and I can understand that Veronica is inwardly close to you. She
is a strange child, as you always were. Perhaps that is
just why I loved you especially. But is that enough
for you? With all that you know and have learned,
can't you undertake other work than just teaching
poor simple-minded Peter?"

"It would be a great work if I were to succeed
in even partially awakening the sleeping spirit in him.
That might be more worth-while than to write great
books. You mustn't look at a mentally retarded person as other people do. You see, we go from life to
life, and if Peter is today an imprisoned soul, he may
once have been a very wise man. It is perhaps out of
pity for the retarded that in this existence he has become retarded himself, so that by experiencing in his
inmost being the sorrows of the backward—their
seeking and finding in all its helplessness—he may
become their leader in a future life."

Ulla Uhlberg looked up astonished.

"I think I could understand that," she said slowly, "but do you believe that Peter was once a wise man?"

"I want to believe it, Ulla. It is at least easier to take the pains I do with him if I accept this as possible. Who can solve the riddle of men's destiny? That is very difficult, and I am not a Master."

"But you knew one?" asked Ulla Uhlberg. "Was that in Asia? Please tell me about it."

"I did indeed know one, but it was not in Asia. How can I say where it was? That is beyond our grasp, Ulla. I learned in Asia what preparation is required to see a Master, but the Master himself I only saw later. It doesn't make any difference where it happens. It doesn't even need to be a person at all in our earthly sense. These are great matters and they are very real, only it is hard to put them into words. You yourself are probably nearer to all this than you imagine, Ulla; otherwise you would not ask about it."

"I do believe that there is a life *behind* material things—a life similar to the one *within* these things. It wouldn't be worth while living if it were not so. I have never been able to believe that this can be all— what people see in their everyday lives and what it means to them. If so, it wouldn't be worth while to go on living and fighting."

"Are you fighting for something, Ulla?"

Ulla Uhlberg bent her head.

"Perhaps, Johannes," she said softly. "We all fight for something, but no one knows if he will win."

Johannes Wanderer was silent and gazed over the flowering splendor of the park, radiant and golden in the midday sun. How closely related was the ripeness of this summer day to Ulla Uhlberg's beauty. But every day must pass its noon and sink to the peace of evening, to night, and to a fresh tomorrow.

"Look, Johannes," continued Ulla Uhlberg, "you spoke of different lives. I understand it this way, that we have lived on this Earth in other forms, that we have returned, and that we shall come back yet again. This is the only way I can explain to myself that destinies link up, work things out together, separate, and meet again. I have given a lot of thought to these things, and I have always been able to understand it. It is much easier for me to grasp than, for instance, ghosts and such supernatural things."

"One doesn't need to be a mystic, Ulla, to understand rebirth. Indeed, from a logical standpoint it is the only possibility of seeing the working out of cause and effect, and justice in everything that happens. That is not to say that one should not help wherever possible, for we ourselves need help and we should bestow help on men, animals, and all life."

"Can you see, Johannes, who a person was before? Or have you ever seen it for anyone in particular?"

"Only very occasionally, Ulla. One can't be too careful. A lot of mischief is done this way, and delusions are perhaps more likely in this than in many other spiritual questions. But the basic thought as such is sound. It brings us again to the view of life that once was close to God, and that is now choked with the sand of materialism."

Ulla Uhlberg had the feeling that Johannes wanted to avoid the issue.

"And what if I should ask you something about this?"

"For instance, who Baron Bombe was?" said Johannes, laughing. "Your ever-faithful admirer, isn't he?"

"Shame on you, Johannes!" cried Ulla Uhlberg. "Don't you have any more attractive example? But while you are about it, *do* you know who he was?"

"I don't think it is worth-while going into that. Such questions demand a great deal of contemplation and quiet, which I wouldn't waste over this problem. People with a primitive pride of rank, and without any intrinsic worth, were mostly insignificant in former lives, and were eaten up by a desire for higher status. They will stay as they are until they learn to free themselves. These are not interesting lives, and it is not worth-while to bother with them. But it is quite true that one can put on these superficial things as one does clothing. The inner tie naturally has laws of its own. I don't want to say anything disagreeable about Baron Bombe. He is amusing and, moreover, he's a harmless creature. One can leave him in peace in the dream of his own excellence."

Ulla Uhlberg laughed.

"I can well imagine Baron Bombe in such an inferior position. He has only changed his clothes, and that is all it seems to be with many people. But there is a lot to be learned in this way, and I often wonder, when I have a dinner party, who all the people really are who are sitting around me wearing their masks of the present day."

"There would often be strange pictures if people took their masks off," said Johannes Wanderer.

"Do you know, Johannes, when I was in Florence it often seemed to me as if everything I saw I had known long ago? I am ashamed to say that I felt more at home there than I do here."

"I can understand that. Yet you came back, Ulla?"

A delicate color flew into Ulla Uhlberg's cheeks.

"Yes; why, Johannes? You of all people must know that this is my home."

She stood up.

"Come, let us go into the park. It is stuffy here. Outside it is lovely among all the flowers."

Johannes Wanderer followed her.

"Did you mean to ask, Ulla, whether I believe that you once lived in Florence? Yes, I do believe it; and you retained much of that life still. Some things one takes on into a later life because they have not yet been worked out. How can I explain that to you, Ulla? It seems to me that you are still clinging to Florence and everything that was there at that time."

"Did you see that, Johannes?"

"I have seen some of it, not all."

"Why does one forget it? There's some remembrance there, but it won't come clear."

"One knew more as a child, Ulla. Veronica too remembers some things. Then one forgets. In the twilight that has fallen, the greatest part of life is only half perceived. It is hard for us, but we have to try

to climb from the darkness up to the light, and what
we then possess is really our own. But until one has
learned that, it is as you say. We forget so easily what
we should not forget, and later it is hard to forget
what we would like to. It is like three candles that all
burn differently until they are even with one another
and unite in one pure flame. Those are life's secrets;
one can only explain them in halting terms. One must
grow into them and let them awaken within oneself."

"Johannes, when I was living in Florence it always seemed to me as if you were standing near me,
and I had the feeling that we had both lived there and
that we were very close to one another, like today,
only perhaps even more. I can't explain just what I
mean."

"We were both in Florence and we were happier
than today, if that is what you mean, but we should
not wish it back. The happiness in Florence was shat-
tered, and it was a ghastly morning when that happened. We have come a great step forward since then,
but we have still further to go and in this we must
help each other, Ulla, you and I. But you mustn't
think so much about Florence. One must go forward
and not back, and we must forget a good deal, believe me."

"So many things are hard to forget, Johannes."

"Certainly, but forgetting doesn't mean that they
are wiped out. Forget the husk that has to fall away,
and keep the inmost kernel of what has happened.
We can make everything easier for ourselves, but
life is hard for everyone who wishes to help, and I

want to help; I am honestly trying to. You too want to help, Ulla, don't you? So many human beings and animals are waiting for help; the world has gone astray, and everywhere there are imprisoned souls."

"I want whatever you want, Johannes," said Ulla Uhlberg simply. "I have you here, and I have caught a piece of Florence in these old walls. Don't you think I have remodeled Irreloh rather well? I was hoping you would feel very happy here, Johannes."

"I like being with you, Ulla, but a castle is not much in my line. I don't want to spoil your pleasure in your possession, and I can see how pretty you have made everything. I can hardly recognize the old ruin that we raved about as children. All the same, I wish you had not bought Irreloh, but had built yourself a new house."

A shadow flitted across Ulla Uhlberg's face.

"I thought you would like Irreloh too. It was the dream of our young days to play knight and enchanted king's daughter here, and you promised to rescue me from the dragon that guarded me. Don't you remember that any more, Johannes?"

"Yes, I know, Ulla. And I will keep my promise. That is why I tell you all this."

Ulla Uhlberg smiled and sat down on a stone garden seat.

"Come, sit by me and tell me what you have against Irreloh. Shall I get rheumatism here, or are there ghosts after all?"

"Look, Ulla, this is what I mean. A human being has a lot in himself—good and bad—according to his

nature and destiny. This has to run its full course and
work itself out. But he also attracts a good many
things to himself from his surroundings. These may
be related to him, or it may be that he lacks the
strength or awareness to defend himself against them.
Therefore I think the choice of a place to live is not
unimportant, provided one is able to choose."

"Is that why you live in the little garden-house,
and not with Regina and Mariechen?"

"Yes, Ulla. I can work better there. Fewer influences reach me. Contemplation is easier, the soil
purer. It seems to me that the bridge to the spiritual
world is a little nearer to me there than in the House
of Shadows."

"Perhaps you are right. Irreloh is not so very
peaceful. Just look at the horrible high tower. Even
my efforts at beautification came to grief there. There's
nothing in it but old rubbish. I only hope now that
the owls will nest there; that would be really roman-
tic. I like owls so much, but they won't oblige me and
live in the old tower. They live round about in the
park. I hear them calling in the night."

"I can understand, Ulla, that the owls won't nest
in the tower. It is not good there. There is a lot not
good in Irreloh."

"What do you mean by that? I'm not afraid of
ghosts."

"I don't mean that there are ghosts. I don't know
about that. I don't know Irreloh as well as the House
of Shadows. What I mean is that in everything there
is something left over from former times, not tangible

of course, but nevertheless real. You know that when a person sensitive to these things takes an object in his hand he can tell what its owner looked like and what his destiny was. I have often experienced that. In this sense there are influences left everywhere, so to speak, but we should not awaken them."

"But I don't, Johannes."

"Perhaps it's more than that. We often have to oppose them, or at least not offer them any encouragement that could link us to them. Here in Irreloh there is much that should not be. Irreloh once had a bad reputation; they lighted false fires on the coast and became rich from the wreckage."

"Oh, but that is a long time ago, Johannes. What has it to do with me? I haven't lighted any false fires or robbed wrecked ships."

Johannes Wanderer shook his head.

"Not you, Ulla, but I meant something different. When I think of myself, I say to myself that there are dangers in me and obscure regions of the soul. We all have somewhere a fire in us that is only too ready to flare up, even if only underneath the ashes, and we have all, often unknowingly, made off with prizes from the wreckage of life. Everything is difficult and strangely interwoven, one thing with another."

"That may well be, Johannes, but I don't want anything but to accept life. If one does that one will surely be able to cope with the old stories."

"That is just what I hope for you: that you accept life in the right way and drive out the ghosts of Irreloh, Ulla. I am not warning you so that you should deny it, certainly not. But have you ever considered how hard it is to accept life? Most people who preach that as a healthy view of the world don't accept life at all; they only accept themselves. They deny life— would they make wars otherwise, kill animals, and destroy whole forests? To accept life means to accept *all* life, reverently to become part of the brotherhood of all creatures. If human beings would do that we should all be happier and better. Today human beings only accept themselves, not life. They deny life, and call it acceptance. The result is chaos. It is not easy, Ulla, really to accept life, so that one accepts all life. It is a real problem if one thinks it out honestly and comes to grips with it."

Ulla Uhlberg gazed wide-eyed at Johannes Wanderer.

"You have thought so much, Johannes; I will gladly learn from you. It is true that today we only speak in catch phrases, and so everything gets more and more confused. And I don't want to deny any other life in accepting mine. I only hope that I shall be successful."

"I will help you, Ulla, as far as I can. Now I must be going home."

"Oh dear! Would you like the carriage?"

"No, thank you; it is not far to the House of Shadows and I like to walk alone."

"You always did, Johannes. But I am afraid you brood over things too much."

"I certainly won't do that. I know it would be a mistake, but I am trying to understand life. Otherwise

I can't help, and help I must; and life is hard to understand."

Ulla Uhlberg bent her lovely head.

"It is indeed. Good-bye, Johannes. Come again soon."

"Good-bye, Ulla. Come and see us too whenever you feel like it. And always be yourself; then you will be mistress over all the ghosts of Irreloh."

Ulla Uhlberg watched Johannes for a long time until he disappeared from her sight on an overgrown forest path. She passed her hand over her forehead.

"Yes, I will be myself," she thought. "Is that hard or easy? Life is certainly different from the way one dreamed it. But whatever it may be, I will accept it. All life is my life too."

She called the groom and had her horse saddled while she changed. She felt in the mood to ride on the heath, and when the horse was dancing under her and the summer wind blowing through her hair she felt again the whole victorious strength of youth, and left the riddles of life and the ghosts of Irreloh far behind her. She rode quickly, and only pulled up when she could see the House of Shadows in the distance.

Three birch trees on the red heath loomed up before her. Then her horse shied and reared. She had trouble in quieting him, and patted him on the neck.

"You don't know anything about what once happened here," she said. "Or can you see more than we can, Hassan?"

Were there shadows everywhere across the paths?

"Come on, Hassan!" she cried, and galloped back

along the road, her eyes fixed on the distance. There life was waiting, and joy stretching into infinity—she was still young, beautiful, and rich, and bore one name on her lips and in her heart.

Hassan galloped, the sparks flying from his hooves.

By the ditch at the side of the road Aaron Mendel was sitting with his pack. Ulla Uhlberg rode by and never saw him.

How many ride on young horses like you, Ulla Uhlberg, gazing into the distance with longing eyes. It is life they are pursuing, life toward which they ride. But often the distance is empty, and you pass life by—life is sitting, quiet and resigned, by the side of the road, bearing its heavy burdens.

*

Veronica had missed Master Mützchen all the afternoon. Mutzeputz didn't know where he was either. Now he suddenly skipped into the playroom and hopped onto Veronica's lap.

"I have been for a trip," he said gaily. "I crept into Uncle Johannes' pocket and went with him to Irreloh. Ordinarily, you know, I am tied to the House of Shadows, and I need some help if I want to go anywhere else. One wants to see something else for a change sometimes."

"Next time I will take you with me in my handbag," said Veronica. "For instance, on Sunday to church in Halmar. Isn't it very dark in Uncle Johannes' pocket?"

"That doesn't matter," said Master Mützchen.

"It is pleasanter there than in Irreloh. That's not a good building, Veronica, and people like me couldn't feel well there. The House of Shadows is much lighter and better to live in, in spite of all its thresholds and steps, and even the Gray Lady's picture book, although that isn't nice at all, seems to me better than the red demons of Irreloh."

"Who are they?" asked Veronica. "They sound pretty spooky."

"Ugh," said Master Mützchen, "they are a disgusting lot. They squat in the old tower tending a fire that they mean to blow up again one day when the right storm and the right hour come from the sea. Who knows when that will be? I wouldn't like to be in it."

"Are they ghosts?" asked Veronica, and she shivered a little.

"No, they are not," said Master Mützchen. "They are worse than that, for one can't talk to them. They are something left over from the false fires, and they have taken shape. It's a bit like the Gray Lady's picture book, only much more horrible, because it has a life of its own. I crept around in the old tower and had a good look at it from all sides. There are three red demons, and they look frightful. Ulla Uhlberg will have to watch out."

"I don't really like Aunt Ulla," said Veronica hesitantly.

"Why not?" asked Master Mützchen, and pricked up his ears like Zottel when something wasn't clear to him.

"Why?" said Veronica. "I don't know. I just don't."

Master Mützchen waggled his ears. He could do that wonderfully, to Veronica's constant joy.

"Then it wasn't very nice at Irreloh?" inquired Veronica.

"Before I went to the tower it was a lot of fun," said Master Mützchen, grinning naughtily. "I crept out of Uncle Johannes' pocket and sat on Pastor Haller's long coat-tails. The Pastor talked a lot, and went on scolding about the superstitions concerning ghosts and little men, just when I was dancing around him."

"Didn't anyone see you?" asked Veronica, laughing.

"Only Uncle Johannes," explained Master Mützchen, "and he told me later that he wouldn't take me with him any more if I was so naughty. But I can't help it if Pastor Haller talks nonsense."

"I will take you along soon in my handbag," Veronica comforted him.

*

Night fell on the gray walls of Irreloh. Ulla Uhlberg slept, and dreamed of flames that consumed her. In the tower squatted the red demons of Irreloh, stirring a flickering fire under the ashes of by-gone times. Shadowy pale figures tapped on the windows, and demanded back the wreckage which had once cost them their lives.

The sea sang in the distance. In the park the owls called.

CHAPTER VI

THE MIRACLE
OF THE TOAD

T was several years later when
the Miracle of the Toad happened. The years that had
passed over the House of Shadows had been quiet,
and there is nothing very much to report about them.
There are various things one might say, perhaps,
about outward existence, such as people going about
their everyday tasks, but this story has to do with the
life behind things. Looking at it with eyes such as
these, one sees only the rare milestones set in the soul
by invisible hands, and it is only their signs and num-
bers that one reads, for it is these which keep their
inner reality across the years. Time is nothing. One
day can be much, and many years but little. Only
where those signposts mark the stages of eternal
growth may one see an indication of something imperishable.

Little Veronica had grown, and she had learned
a lot of things she had not known before. It is true
that she did not go to school, because Dr. Gallus
thought it was not good for her and she was still very

delicate, but her mother and Uncle Johannes had been giving her lessons. She was very proud that she now knew something of what people called knowledge. But at the same time it is quite certain that she had forgotten something of what she had known earlier. The great twilight, which had come down upon her for the first time in the Garden of Spirits, had widened around her, and its shadows veiled from her much that she had once taken for granted about existence.

Veronica saw the Gray Lady very seldom now, when she drifted through the House of Shadows and suddenly appeared in a dark corner for a moment, only to vanish again mysteriously. She always gave Veronica a friendly smile, but only spoke a few words. Perhaps, though, Veronica did not understand her silent thought-speech as clearly now as before. But she continued to be anxious about Veronica.

"Don't fall, Little Veronica," she urged her repeatedly. "I fell here too; there are so many steps and thresholds in the House of Shadows."

Veronica nodded, and looked at the Gray Lady wide-eyed.

Only once she asked: "Haven't you been over that threshold yet that you want to cross?"

Then the Gray Lady had shaken her head, looking very sad.

"It must grow light first in Halmar church," she said.

Veronica did not ask her again. It depressed her; she found it hard to understand, and she was quite glad she only saw the Gray Lady so seldom.

You must not think that Little Veronica had become like most children when they slip over into this world as adults. Veronica was a very old soul, and had experienced too much on the long journeys of former lives to be capable of forgetting everything. She could still, as always, talk with Mutzeputz and Zottel, and she still took Master Mützchen's advice as before. She now carried Master Mützchen around with her quite often in her handbag, especially on Sunday when she went to Halmar church, and she enjoyed it when Mutzchen stuck his funny face with its waggling ears and red hat out of her bag. This made a welcome change if Pastor Haller, as he usually did, preached a rather boring sermon. And it was fun to think that no one else noticed Master Mützchen.

But at other times, for instance when the girls of Halmar refused to take Master Mützchen seriously, she was very much annoyed. Though Veronica did not have any real school friends because she did not go to Halmar school, her mother had wanted her to know other girls, and it vexed Veronica very much that they did not want to know anything about Master Mützchen, and laughingly explained him away as a joke on her part. So the acquaintance never became any closer, and was even less close because the Halmar girls looked upon Mutzeputz as just a cat and Zottel as just a dog, not as personalities of worth and dignity. Veronica had had to overcome a feeling of loneliness, not yet too painfully clear, of course, for she lived in a secure home and was certainly not alone. But it was the first presentiment of how lonely people may become who look behind tangible things, and how far they move from those other people who only walk the noisy streets of outward life.

So Veronica drew apart somewhat, and it was only slow-witted Peter who remained always her faithful playmate. The girls had laughed at Peter too, and that Veronica could never forgive them. You could understand perhaps that other people couldn't see Master Mützchen—he was so thin and transparent, because he didn't eat anything. You could find it excusable in the circumstances that people not familiar with Mutzeputz and Zottel didn't think as much of them as those who knew them better undoubtedly did. But that anyone could laugh at Peter because he found it hard to understand so many things—that was brutal, and she valiantly placed herself on guard before her simple childhood companion. Certainly other people knew more, but Peter believed. Wasn't believing a power too, perhaps a greater one? It is true that other people understood better than Peter did the everyday kind of things everyone understands, but didn't Peter grasp everything she told him about Mutzeputz and Zottel and Master Mützchen, or about the Gray Lady's picture book? Deep inside her Veronica understood how much nearer to the meaning of life Peter was, how much nearer he was to herself, to animals, to flowers, and to another world that was greater, brighter, and more real than Halmar with its narrow streets and dark houses.

And Peter adored her. Wasn't it wonderful to be adored? There were some people she adored and looked up to too, for instance Mutzeputz and Uncle Johannes.

The many live outwardly, the few inwardly, and so people who ought to be finding and helping each other grow apart. Confusion has fallen upon our time, and souls pass each other by. You who walk the Earth today, remember this: a turning point has come for the world, and ways are parting. They lead steeply to the sunlit heights, or down to the valleys of the deep. It is not good as it is, and the Earth has become dangerously dark. It has perhaps never been so dark as now. You who are living today, think of the Morningland of Mankind and learn to seek and find it again. Cast light through the houses of shadows, so that you may live again in temples and light-filled mansions, as once in some first morning of the world. It is the Spirit of Pentecost that is calling to you, and that you have forgotten. Pentecost has drawn near again. Will you not comprehend it?

It was a few days before Pentecost when the Miracle of the Toad happened, and I must tell you about it because in Little Veronica's life it became a new milestone inscribed in letters and signs of gold.

It was growing toward evening, and the sun was getting low. Johannes Wanderer and Peter were working on a flowerbed in the garden, and Veronica was helping them, though rather listlessly. She did not feel like doing much today; it was an odd lassitude, but it was only physical. In her spirit everything was more alive than usual, and it seemed to her as if she were freed from the ground and was off walking somewhere in the garden, while actually she was sitting with Uncle Johannes and Peter by the flowerbed, thoughtfully letting the seeds trickle through her fingers. Perhaps it was the Spirit of Pentecost that made everything around her today more transparent and clear, and allowed her once again to hear such strange voices. These rang in her ears, well known and familiar, as if they had once spoken to her already on some far-off day. Didn't it seem today as if the garden were again a Garden of Spirits? When had it last been like this? She did not remember. The way she felt now, it seemed to her like an awakening and a remembrance of her own being.

"Uncle Johannes," said Veronica, "so many thoughts are talking to me. It's been a long time since I heard voices like these in the garden, as I do today."

"Everything that exists is a thought," said Johannes Wanderer, "and all thoughts speak and form themselves into substance, good and bad. We are near Pentecost, Veronica, and in all life the Spirit is stronger than usual. That is why it is clearer to you what the trees are whispering about and what the flowers hold secretly in their cups. The animals, too, sense the holy days of the world. Don't you see that Master Mützchen's red hat is glowing extra brightly, and that Mutzeputz and Zottel are more joyous than usual?"

Indeed it was true that Master Mützchen's hat gleamed with striking effect in the sun. Mützchen was balancing himself carefully and solemnly as he passed a bed of radishes, and it seemed to Veronica as if the radishes were laughing at him.

"Don't take offense, Mützchen," she called to him, "radishes are always a bit pert and sharp-tongued."

Master Mützchen behaved as if none of this had any effect on him. What had the radishes to do with him? He was far above such things.

"Look, Veronica," said Johannes Wanderer. "When I put the seed into the earth, it grows and gets bigger all the time; it forms a stem, leaves and buds; and then a blossom, which in turn holds many new seeds. All this is there already in the seed; it is the thought of the flower which transforms itself into substance. And so is every living thing a thought of God, and remains such a thought even when the substance in its individual shapes falls into decay. The *essence* of thought alone is real in everything, and what it forms is only its changing expression. Is that clear?"

"Yes," said Veronica. "But what about our own thoughts? Are they real too, and do they turn into shapes around us as well?"

"Yes, of course, Veronica, and that's why it is so important to have good and right thoughts. Each person creates his own spiritual surroundings. With many people these don't look at all pretty, and the dark forces that are related to these images hang onto them. But a good thought not only protects you yourself and helps your being to grow into the light.

It is, at the same time, a power which reaches out farther. Through every thought of goodness, a wicked
person becomes better, a wild animal less savage, and
a poisonous plant less dangerous. There is a rise and
fall woven together in everything, and the whole of
creation, now sunk in darkness, is striving together
upward to the light and longs for knowledge and deliverance. Everything that happens here, however
outwardly tangible, originated in a thought. Pentecost
is very near, Veronica, and a piece of the Earth will
once more become spiritualized."

Peter listened, but did not say a word. He had to
take in and absorb everything he heard very slowly.
But he planted one seed reverently beside another.

Mutzeputz and Zottel were playing on a garden
path. From time to time Mutzeputz boxed Zottel's ear
with a velvet paw.

"Please be careful," Veronica said to him. "I
have a feeling it is quite near here that the beetles
have their country-houses. I believe I saw one once."

"Of course you saw it," said Mutzeputz, jumping
over Zottel's back in a single bound, "but it really
wasn't worth talking about. However, we'll be a little
careful because that is what you'd like and because it
is just about Pentecost."

"Do you know that too?" asked Veronica.

"What don't I know?" said Mutzeputz grandly.

"Yes, you certainly do know a lot," said Veronica, full of admiration.

A hedgehog rustled in the undergrowth. You

could only see a flash of something prickly disappearing. Zottel rushed after it, but Veronica called him back.

"It was good of you, Veronica," said the Hedgehog, "to call Zottel back. We can't stand being barked at in such a vulgar way. And I won't bear you a grudge for once calling my children balls."

Veronica thought this over. When was it? When had she said this? She felt as if a veil were slowly becoming transparent, and dimly through it a picture she had once seen took shape.

"I once made some very derogatory remarks about Mutzeputz," called a blackbird to Veronica from a tree. "We nearly parted company over it. I won't say that I take back my opinion entirely, but I must admit that Mutzeputz respected our sanctuary when you fed us at your window in the winter. We are much obliged, too, for the fare you provided. It was good and plentiful, and I have recommended you to my friends. A few of the seeds seemed a little hard, but that might have been in the crops. I won't say it was the fault of your catering establishment."

"What extraordinary things I'm hearing today," thought Veronica, "and everyone seems to be in a much more peaceful and friendly mood. Is this something of the Spirit of Pentecost too that is talking in nature?"

Veronica mused over this.

"Uncle Johannes," she said, "it really looks as if everything has the feeling that a holy day is near."

"It is a premonition that the whole world will

one day have peace and holy days. That is what we are living and working for, Veronica."

Now Veronica saw that Master Mützchen was playing with a colored butterfly. The butterfly fluttered its wings, and Master Mützchen waggled his ears and kept bowing in the oddest way. How funny it looked. Oh no, it wasn't a butterfly after all; it was a delicate transparent being with butterfly wings. Hadn't she seen this little sylph once before? Yes, she had— he nodded to her. And now he flew up, his colored wings spread wide in the blue air.

Over everything lay a great and sun-drenched stillness. Only in the distance there were black clouds, and sheet lightning flashed in them.

It was peace. But warfare lurked within it.

A raucous voice startled Veronica.

"Just you wait, you hideous beast! I'm going to kill you!"

Veronica turned around with a start, and Johannes Wanderer and Peter looked up quickly from their work. Near them stood the gardener's man, Eriksen from Halmar, with his hoe raised threateningly. Veronica rushed up to him. She arrived just in time to save from Eriksen's blow a large toad which was crawling slowly along the ground. The blood rushed into Veronica's face.

"Leave the toad alone!" she cried furiously.

"It's nothing to do with you," said Eriksen angrily, but he lowered the hoe.

He could not strike, for Veronica stood in front of the toad to protect it.

Then Johannes Wanderer and Peter came up.

"Let the toad go, Eriksen," said Johannes Wanderer quietly. "Veronica is right. The toad is not doing anyone any harm."

"It's loathsome, and anyway I'm mad at everything today."

It was obvious that Eriksen had been drinking.

"The toad is not loathsome," said Johannes Wanderer. "As a matter of fact it has beautiful eyes. Anyway, we are not going to let you do anything to it."

The toad had stopped crawling, and now sat on the ground panting. Was it exhausted from shock, or did it sense that it had been saved? Perhaps both.

"I can kill the vermin if I want to," shouted Eriksen angrily.

"You are here to do your work in the garden, nothing else," said Johannes Wanderer. "We don't take anyone into our garden to kill animals."

"Can I go then?"

"As you please," said Johannes Wanderer, "but I would rather you understood that you were in the wrong. The toad is also a creature, like the rest of us. It wants to live too."

Veronica had stepped back, and the two men stood facing one another. There was something threatening in their attitude.

"Take a good look at that, Veronica," said a gentle little voice coming from the tree. "You once wanted to see the great ones who stand behind the dwarfs when they quarrel. You have protected life,

Veronica, and now you have won a little of the eyes of the depths. Look at that, Veronica. That is the battleground of Light and Dark. More is at stake than a poor frightened toad. It is the redemption of the world that is at stake, the awakening of Snow White in the glass coffin."

Yes, it must be; it really was the Elf in the tree, and now Veronica looked. What she saw was tremendous, and at the same time it was ghastly. Evidently Master Mützchen, Mutzeputz, and Zottel saw the same thing too, for Mützchen's thin legs trembled, Mutzeputz spat, and Zottel's hackles rose.

Johannes Wanderer and Eriksen spoke not a word. But there was bitter strife between them. Veronica saw it clearly. She was watching it with the eyes of the depths. Both men bore arms, but these were not material. Eriksen had a crude, heavy club in his hand, and Johannes a sword, and he was clad from head to foot in silver armor. On his helmet was a cross. Veronica had never seen him wearing this. And neither man was alone. Behind Eriksen stood many dark and terrible figures armed as he was, who urged him on. But at Johannes' side stood a host of knights in silver armor with drawn swords. They were followed by others wearing even more resplendent armor. Between the two hosts the toad squatted, frightened and helpless.

The distant black clouds had approached, a dazzling blue streak of lightning flashed, and the thunder growled threateningly.

Veronica shivered. She had grasped something of the great battle of the spirits in this world and the other.

Now Johannes Wanderer took a stride forward, and Eriksen and the shadowy figures fell back.

Slowly the picture faded.

"Why should I let others live?" said Eriksen bitterly. "My child is sick, and God doesn't help him either."

"I didn't know that," replied Johannes Wanderer, and it was as if slowly, step by step, he pressed Eriksen away from the dark ones. "I am very sorry your child is sick; I will come and see him. But do you believe God will help him sooner if you destroy life, instead of respecting it?"

Eriksen thought this over for a long time.

"Perhaps you are right," he said. He laid down the hoe and left the garden.

The others said nothing and went back to their work. The black clouds moved off, and only in the distance the thunder growled. The evening deepened, and the sun went down in a fiery glow.

For a long time Veronica stood without speaking, gazing wide-eyed into the light.

"Uncle Johannes," she said softly, "it looks just as if I could see a castle in the red clouds—a castle with high towers and battlements."

Then Johannes Wanderer laid his gardening tools aside.

"You see it today for the first time because you have protected life," he said solemnly. "Hold the pic-

ture of this castle in your soul, Veronica. What you
see is Montsalvat."

Veronica folded her hands involuntarily.

"I believe I've heard that name before," she said,
awe-struck.

"You have heard it and you will hear it again,
Veronica."

Mutzeputz and Zottel were sitting motionless.
Master Mützchen had taken his red hat off, which he
seldom did, and Peter stared reverently and helplessly
into the glow.

"Can you see it too?" whispered Veronica.

The poor boy shook his head sadly.

"I see nothing, but I believe it," he said with
reverence, and this time there was a deep inner misery
in his voice.

Johannes Wanderer bent down to him.

"You mustn't be sad, Peter, if you can't see it.
You believe it, and you must think that there are so
many things God doesn't let you see yet because He
has a special joy in your great faith."

Then a smile spread over the boy's face, and in
him was an infinite peace.

For a little while still they gazed into the glow
of the sun. Then they gathered their gardening tools
together in silence and went into the House of Shadows.

"Uncle Johannes," said Veronica, "I saw you
wearing silver armor today, and behind you there
were a lot of others. Do they all come from Montsalvat?"

"Yes, Veronica," said Johannes Wanderer. "It will be a hard fight on this Earth until it is flooded with light and sunshine."

"The silver armor is beautiful," said Veronica.

"And yet those who wear it are only fighters of modest rank," said Johannes Wanderer. "Behind them stand much greater knights, but they very seldom come down to an earthly journey. Here we are erring human beings, and we wear armor only when we hold our shield over the weak and defenseless. This has to do with the Quest of the Grail."

"I would like to wear silver armor like that," said Veronica.

"It may well be that God has sent you to Earth again just so that you should wish this," said Johannes Wanderer.

The sun went down. In the distance the bells of Halmar sounded for eventide.

Pentecost was approaching.

*

The next morning Johannes Wanderer went into Halmar to visit Eriksen and ask after his sick child. Eriksen came to meet him at the door.

"I want to apologize for yesterday, Mr. Johannes," said he haltingly. "I was wrong, but I had the feeling that there was someone standing behind me—someone stronger than myself. Man is weak, Mr. Johannes; he often doesn't know what he is doing or saying."

"Of course, Eriksen, I understand that. And it

is a great satisfaction to me that you think differently today. We will forget it now. I only came to ask after your sick child."

"My child has recovered," said Eriksen.

He was very pale, and his voice shook noticeably.

"It happened this way, Mr. Johannes," he went on. "In the middle of the night he got better quite suddenly. The fever left him, and the child woke and told me—Mr. Johannes, we must believe it if the child said so himself—he had dreamed that a large toad had come to him and had made him quite well. The child laughed and was very happy, but I didn't laugh, Mr. Johannes. Something stuck in my throat as I heard it. It is a miracle, Mr. Johannes, and I haven't deserved it."

"There are many mysteries in the things that happen, Eriksen; let us be grateful for them even though we don't understand them."

"I am grateful, God knows," said Eriksen, "but do you really believe that this toad healed my child? Such a poor, weak creature, and yet somehow this must be true."

"You must remember that all toads draw their life from one spirit common to them all, and that this spirit must be strong, as you may well imagine. It stands as near to the individual toad as it itself does to God, for God is in it and in the frightened toad of yesterday."

"We are weak and ignorant people, Mr. Johannes, but we are not so bad as not to believe in God and in miracles. This is a miracle. Thanks be to

God that I have experienced it. Life is harsh and difficult—what would it be like if no miracles took
place? I am certainly going to tell everyone in Halmar
about the Miracle of the Toad. I know they'll believe
me, for the people of Halmar know little but believe
a lot. It is only Pastor Haller who doesn't believe in
miracles. He says these are only tales, and the important thing is for us to live according to Christ. But
we want to believe in miracles, Mr. Johannes; all the
modern things don't mean anything to us. We can't
get through life just with them only. And for a long
time we have meant to tell the Pastor that we can't
use his new-fangled stuff in Halmar. Yes indeed, we
are going to tell him straightaway—and I shall be the
first of all, for I have seen the Miracle of the Toad."

While talking, Eriksen had worked himself up
into a state of passionate conviction, and it was quite
true that the voice of Halmar spoke through him;
Johannes Wanderer knew that well.

"You are right, Eriksen," he said kindly, "but
won't you be a little more patient and wait until the
Pastor of Halmar experiences a miracle himself? I am
sure this would be better and more peaceful."

"I want to see what he has to say to the Miracle
of the Toad," said Eriksen stubbornly.

Johannes Wanderer left, and Eriksen told all the
people of Halmar about the Miracle of the Toad. The
people believed him, and since that day the animals
in Halmar have had a better life than before.

So the Miracle of the Toad went on working, like
every thought of goodness.

Johannes Wanderer reported to Veronica on the Miracle of the Toad, quietly and in very simple words. Veronica found it completely understandable. She herself had had a very strange experience the same night. For a long time she had not been able to sleep, and gazed into the distance with wakeful inner eyes. Outside, the storm had returned; the thunder rolled, and blue lightning flashed in the dark, menacing clouds. There Veronica saw how the sun of Pentecost shone through the warring darkness and sketched a golden fairy-tale crown on the head of the toad.

Veronica beheld even more than that. She saw that Snow White in the glass coffin opened her eyes and smiled—and she heard in storm and thunder the clash of weapons. There stood the fighters of Montsalvat. And for Veronica it was as if the Grail had summoned her too to its banner.

CHAPTER VII

THE DEAD IN THE CHURCH OF HALMAR

HIS is a story of this world and the other, and that is why I must tell you about the dead in the church of Halmar. For it is a fact that the dead are not snuffed out, as many believe in these days that have strayed further from spiritual things than almost any former time. The dead live on in the whole essence of their being, only changing a coarse garment for a finer one, and the world which they enter through the curtained doorway is far more real than the world of appearances we live in on this Earth. It is not true, either, that the two worlds are separated by an insurmountable wall. Only a thin veil hangs between them, and it lifts much more often than people of today believe. There are many moments when this world and the other merge, so that we cannot say whether we are here or over there.

For the dead help us in the building of the Earth, and they wish so very much that the living would work hand in hand with them again as did the men of bygone days. Is not many an idea that we have the thought of someone who has died, and a feeling that comes over us the wish and will of spirits close to us? The dead help us, and we should help them. If that does not happen, the world will become a wasteland and the plaything of the dark forces. But it must be filled with light, together with all who live on it, until it reaches that eternal peace which will be a Sunday of the world. That will take a long time—today is a working day, and the holy day is still far off.

You who walk the Earth today, think of this and do not disown the dead who stand near you. The dead are just as diverse as the living; there are light and dark among them, and they are with you in your light and your dark doings. Therefore take care that your words and deeds are filled with light, for what you speak and do is for this world and the other, for the living and for the dead, and for the building of the whole world. There are so many dead who want to help you—do not pass them by. And too, there are so many dead who need your help—do not deny it to them. There are many dead far above you in the heights; there are also many in the valleys of the deep, and there are also those who cannot cross the threshold because it is dark around them and they cannot comprehend the other world. They drift through your houses of shadows and seek in your churches. But today they find little enough light, because it has become very dark on the Earth in this turning point of time.

Think of this, you who walk the Earth today. Let your mansions and your temples become light for the living and for the dead, so that the two worlds merge again into the Morningland of Mankind. Do you not see yourselves how dark it has become around you? Does not the Gray Lady wander through the rooms of the House of Shadows, year after year, and are there not many other dead searching in the narrow streets of Halmar and listening for the bells when they ring for Sunday? But there are no holy days any more with you, and it is dark in the church of Halmar.

Light your candles! So many are waiting for it to become light again. The living and the dead are calling for it; men, animals, and all things that exist long for light and deliverance. The hours that strike today are hours of destiny for the world; great light is needed, for it has become much too dark. I must tell you this, and I must try to light for you candle after candle so that you truly understand when I tell you about the dead in the church of Halmar. You may think: these are old tales, and who knows if they are true? But, believe me, they are tales that can become true again any day. For the dead are standing beside you.

*

It had been the custom for years to mark Aunt Mariechen's birthday with great ceremony in the House of Shadows, and friends and acquaintances gathered there, for she was the oldest of them all and stood for everything that was domestic in the present-day sense. Aunt Mariechen always considered this celebration of special importance. She baked mountains of cakes so that not one of her guests should go away hungry, and this had certainly never happened for as long as anyone could remember.

Peter and Zottel appeared as the first guests, but they stayed most of the time in the playroom because Peter did not like to be among strangers. Today many had already come and left again. Now they were sitting in the big gallery next to the Green Room: Ulla Uhlberg next to Johannes Wanderer, Pastor Haller and his wife, and Dr. Gallus. Regina was rather reserved as always, Aunt Mariechen a little excited, and Veronica divided her time between the guests and Peter in the playroom. Master Mützchen followed her faithfully, while Mutzeputz, annoyed at so much disturbance of his peace, only glanced into the front hall when a new guest appeared. He did not like noise and bustle in the house and looked unmistakably disapproving.

Pastor Haller was also out of humor today, although he had nothing else in common with Mutzeputz. On the contrary, the philosophical outlook that Mutzeputz possessed in such abundance was entirely lacking in Pastor Haller, and today more than ever, because he was annoyed about the rumors of the alleged "toad miracle" that Eriksen had been pestering him with.

"It is out of the question that I should, in the name of the Church so to speak, countenance such superstitions. I could put up with them and even look the other way, but Eriksen practically demanded that I recognize his harebrained theories about miracles and, what is worse, he is infecting the people of Halmar, who in any case are inclined to believe such flimsy tales."

"I don't mind at all if toads practice medicine," said Dr. Gallus, indifferent to the Pastor's injured feelings. "Then I shall have someone to take my place when I retire. Hrrr-mph!"

"The toad is not supposed to have practiced medicine, Doctor," put in Johannes Wanderer. "It is only claimed that it healed. You must be fair and admit that these are two different things. Why should not a toad heal without practicing medicine? There are doctors who practice without healing."

Dr. Gallus snapped his jaws together like a beak.

"One can never tell with you if you are good-natured or sarcastic, just like my parrot."

"I didn't mean to say anything unkind, Doctor," said Johannes Wanderer, "especially not about you. I know that you have healed, and I shall never forget how gentle you were with poor Peter when he was ill. Let us leave the practice of medicine for the moment. Don't you think, for instance, that you set a force in motion when you care for a sick person with your whole sympathy, when you disregard trouble and inconvenience that perhaps often cost you a very real sacrifice? You are no longer so very young, and yet you are available day and night. Don't you think that such a force also carries help and healing in itself, often more so than a prescription? Healing is an art, and as such is spiritual and not mechanical, as is believed in some decadent quarters of modern medicine.

But if your art is incalculable, can there not be other powers hard to estimate which are in some way connected with a poor hunted toad? Moreover, this is said to have happened in sleep. Where are we when we sleep? Sleep is another world. Science knows nothing about it, and yet it is almost half our lives."

"You may be right," said Dr. Gallus; "we all only know a little, and we don't know what the power is that heals. I can't follow you entirely, but then I don't understand everything that my parrot says. As a matter of fact you remind me of my parrot, Mr. Johannes."

"Many people say the same about you, Doctor," said Johannes Wanderer. "But to me personally this comparison is not at all disagreeable. I am very fond of your parrot."

"Is that so?" snapped Dr. Gallus. "Do people say that? Well, they are right. My parrot has more sense than all the people of Halmar put together. But now I must go. My patients are calling for me. I am sorry, but those are the 'incalculable forces' that I have to reckon with. We will hope that they transform themselves into healing powers."

Dr. Gallus took his leave, and Johannes Wanderer accompanied him to the door.

"This Pastor Haller with his textbook of morals is a donkey," growled Dr. Gallus angrily. "He should be glad that the people of Halmar still believe in miracles, for if Halmar is to get used to him that would have to be a miracle in itself."

"He practices without healing," said Johannes

Wanderer. "That is usual today because people don't know about the incalculable forces any more."

Dr. Gallus meant to make another biting remark, but he collided with Baron Bombe in the doorway and hastily took his departure.

Baron Bombe's whole make-up was coarse and countrified. He cast a disparaging glance at Mutzeputz, who immediately turned his back on him and withdrew. Noisy people disgusted his cultural sensibilities. Baron Bombe entered the drawing room and greeted everyone beamingly. His little pale-blue eyes had spotted Ulla Uhlberg, toward whom he displayed an ostentatious devotion.

"A good thing that the cat outside didn't cross my path. I can't bear cats. Dogs and horses are different. I like strength, don't you, dear lady?"

Baron Bombe almost barked, as primitive people with a pronounced sense of self-importance are apt to do.

"He has insulted Mutzeputz," said Veronica; "I won't say 'how do you do' to him."

"Veronica," her mother whispered to her, "please behave or you will have to leave the room."

Veronica retired to a corner, and fortunately Baron Bombe did not notice her.

"I only like strength that is refined and polished," said Ulla Uhlberg evasively; "that's why I like cats and cultured people."

Veronica forgot at this moment that she really didn't like Ulla Uhlberg. Baron Bombe only dimly understood his snub and laughed bleatingly, though he seemed a little self-conscious. Aunt Mariechen poured him some coffee and plied him with so many cakes that he could have lived on them for a considerable time.

"We were just talking about the people of Halmar and their superstitions," remarked Regina diplomatically, to lead the dangerous conversation about the culture of cats and people into other channels. The Miracle of the Toad did not seem to her in any way conclusive. She was less inclined than Johannes to let it stand. Admittedly she was not clear about it, and she wavered in her opinion as she nearly always did.

"Superstitions? Splendid!" cried Baron Bombe. "The people here believe anything you like. An ideal parish for you, Pastor, isn't it?"

Baron Bombe looked at Pastor Haller with hearty goodwill.

"That it definitely is not," said Pastor Haller, tight-lipped. "I simply cannot come to terms with the sentiments of the people here, and I am seriously considering getting transferred to a large town where they are more up-to-date."

"Oh," said Baron Bombe, "but it is delightful here."

"And there is a movement against my husband in Halmar, too," Mrs. Haller explained sadly.

"Yes," said Pastor Haller with irritation, "they are coming to see me tomorrow about these things, a sort of Church Council I imagine. But I have no intention of sanctioning their nonsense. I shall simply tell them that I have had enough and am leaving."

"But, Harald dear," said Mrs. Haller soothingly.

Aunt Mariechen handed him the plate of cakes, and Baron Bombe tried to assist her politely. In this attempt the coffee cup in his hand began to wobble and spilled its contents irretrievably over him. Baron Bombe was tall and broad, and the coffee traced the widest possible path across his white vest. Regina and Aunt Mariechen rushed to help him.

"Mutzeputz has never spilled anything on *his* white vest," announced Veronica with triumphant satisfaction.

"Veronica, leave the room," said her mother, trying by her zealous efforts on Baron Bombe's vest to wipe away the impression of these devastating words.

But Baron Bombe was entirely concerned with himself and his mishap. Such a thing happened to him very seldom, and now it had to happen just when Ulla Uhlberg was present. Certainly she looked sympathetic, but that might be hypocrisy.

"This can happen to anyone, and when it happens to me, then it always happens several times in a row," comforted Aunt Mariechen.

But Baron Bombe remained downcast and took his leave soon afterwards. He felt unsure of himself in his stained vest, and it was not to be borne that he should appear anything but victorious.

He had hardly left when Veronica appeared again. She behaved as though nothing had happened, although she brought Peter with her as a safeguard. Peter would take people's minds off her, and everyone inquired how he was. He was rather at a loss, but assured them he was well.

Regina called Veronica to her. She was looking too pleased after this painful incident.

"Veronica, you must not make such remarks."

"Oh, that," said Veronica. "Why did he insult Mutzeputz? I told Mutzeputz, Peter, and Zottel that Baron Bombe had spilled the coffee over his white vest, and they were all delighted. The Gray Lady was standing near, and even she laughed a little. She must have been very pleased. I have never seen her laugh before."

"Good Heavens, does the child believe in ghosts too?" said Pastor Haller, scandalized. "Do you dream many things of this kind, Veronica?"

"The child often has ideas," said Aunt Mariechen, troubled. To have ideas struck Aunt Mariechen as highly suspect.

Veronica had the feeling that the Gray Lady was threatened. They were a queer company today. First Mutzeputz was attacked, and now the Gray Lady. All she needed was for someone to say something derogatory about Master Mützchen.

"I didn't dream it; I saw it," Veronica said defiantly. "When I dream it is quite different, but then it is often very real too, as it was the other night."

"What did you dream the other night, dear?" asked Mrs. Haller kindly.

It seemed to her that her husband had been too harsh with Veronica. He was too harsh altogether, in her view. Her father had been different, much gentler and more patient. Dear God, why shouldn't one take a little interest in the dreams of children? Dreaming ends soon enough—and for her it had ended long ago.

Veronica hesitated a moment.

"I dreamed that Christ was standing on the high-road and lifted the heavy pack from old Aaron Mendel. Christ looked just like the picture in my bedroom."

There was silence for a while. Nobody knew what to say.

"That is a beautiful dream," said Pastor Haller finally, hesitating; "all the more so since Aaron Mendel is a Jew."

Veronica looked him straight in the face.

"It wasn't an ordinary dream. It is real when I dream like that. And Christ didn't ask whether Aaron Mendel was a Jew."

At that Pastor Haller lowered his eyes.

"You are right, Veronica," said Johannes Wanderer, and Ulla Uhlberg nodded to her.

"Do you dream such beautiful things too?" Mrs. Haller asked Peter.

"No," said Peter, "but I believe it."

"Shall we go into the garden?" suggested Aunt Mariechen.

This spiritual conversation might be edifying, but it seemed to her a little too serious for a birthday party. Besides, one never knows if people will quarrel over these things, and Aunt Mariechen certainly did not want that. She was always for the middle path and peace and comfort.

They all stood up to go into the garden, but they were rather silent. Pastor Haller held Johannes Wanderer back a moment in the house. He looked pale and was obviously struggling with himself.

"It seems to me," he began softly, "that this young girl and this feeble-minded boy are better Christians than I."

"Yes," said Johannes Wanderer calmly.

"This comes as a surprise to me. It is very upsetting. Perhaps you understand that," said Pastor Haller uncertainly. "I must come to a decision, but now I really don't know what to do. Perhaps you can advise me? Shall I stay in Halmar and try again, or shall I decide for a big town? Which road shall I take?"

"As regards the external solution I cannot advise you; the inner one I told you of once, Pastor, some years ago. You didn't listen. There is only one road: the Road to Damascus."

Pastor Haller twisted his fingers nervously together and looked into the distance.

"I will try," he said.

*

In the evening when they were alone Veronica turned to Johannes Wanderer.

"Uncle Johannes," she said, "do you know what the best thing of all was today? Baron Bombe didn't spill the coffee over his white vest, Master Mützchen did it. Did you see him upset the cup? I still laugh when I think about it."

"I didn't see it, Veronica; I was thinking of other things. But it was very naughty of Master Mützchen."

Veronica shook her head.

"You mustn't say that, Uncle Johannes. Remember, Baron Bombe insulted Mutzeputz."

"I remember that," said Johannes Wanderer, "but the punishment was rather harsh. Of course one must say for Master Mützchen that it is good to stand up for one's friends."

"Yes, isn't it? I should have upset the coffee myself if I could have. Oh, it was lovely!" said Veronica.

Mutzeputz sat in state in a big armchair, blinking at them with half-shut eyes. He looked as if he were laughing.

Pastor Haller did not sleep that night. He sat alone in his study until dawn, and he never told anyone a word of the thoughts that passed through his mind that lonely night.

In the morning the people of Halmar came, as they had previously announced, to speak to the Pastor. They clumped in noisily, and their expressions were dogged and morose. Eriksen was at their head and was evidently to be their spokesman. Pastor Haller invited them to sit down. He remained standing at his desk. He looked pale and as if he had not slept.

"I know what you want to say," he began, "but it will be better if you let me speak first. I believe then nothing more will be needed and that you will be satisfied. You wish to say that I have not been to you

the Pastor that you need and that you want. You are
quite right. You wanted to go your old ways and I
tried to lead you into other ways. I was wrong. I see
that now, and I am sorry. I have taken trouble, but it
was not the right trouble, for you were nearer to
Christ than I. Now I have come nearer to him. You
are also right when you believe in miracles. Miracles
happen every day. I didn't know that. I know it now
for I have experienced a miracle myself. I am not
ready to be your Pastor; you must have a better one,
and I will help you to find him. I have said that I
would go to a big town. I shall not do that; I will go
to a much smaller place than Halmar to learn, so that
one day perhaps I may become Pastor of Halmar
again. We will not say any more but will part in great
peace, and you will forgive me if I have not done
rightly by you."

The men of Halmar rose from their seats one
after another. There was a great silence among them.
Nothing was to be heard but the birds singing in the
garden outside. Finally Eriksen spoke, twisting his hat
nervously in his fingers.

"You are right, Reverend Haller, sir," he said;
"we are very sinful men. But we will improve, indeed
we will."

Pastor Haller passed his hand over his forehead.

"You did not understand me," he said wearily,
"I was not speaking of your sins but of mine, and I
have asked your forgiveness so that we may part in
peace. That is all."

"We understood you very well, Reverend," said

Eriksen. "We didn't expect you to speak in this way, sir. When you speak like this, you are much better than we are, sir. You can speak of your fault because you have overcome it, and so when you speak this way you are really speaking of our fault. We understand that only too well, and we are sinful men. We would like to say too that we are very sorry."

"Don't let us make it harder for ourselves than it is," said Pastor Haller, "it is hard enough for me, but now we must be honest and sincere, and it will certainly be best as I have suggested—best for you, for I will do all in my power that it shall be the best for you. Then when peace comes at the end I shall have been for once really the Pastor of Halmar."

Eriksen kept on twisting his hat in his hands.

"We would like to beg you, sir, to remain as Pastor in Halmar. That is why we are standing here. We know that we shall never get a better Pastor in Halmar. So, Reverend Haller, sir, you must remain in Halmar."

Harald Haller struggled with a tremendous emotion.

"I thank you very much indeed," he said. "I will do that."

*

The following morning the church in Halmar was crowded. There was not a single seat to be had. Pastor Haller preached as he had never preached before. He spoke of the light that shines in the darkness; he spoke of the miracles that occur day by day for those who have learned to see them, and he said that we must help to bear one another's burdens as Christ did and as Christ still does today.

It was very still in the church of Halmar, and when Pastor Haller left, as many as could reach him grasped his hand.

Then he turned and walked home alone. But he was not alone. Someone spoke beside him, or it seemed to him as if someone was speaking in him.

"You don't know who is speaking to you," said the voice, "because you don't see anyone. But you know now that the invisible is as real as the visible. It is the Gray Lady from the House of Shadows who is walking beside you. I want to thank you, Harald Haller, for today it has become light in the church of Halmar, and light has come to many who longed for it. You are glad that your church was full, but it was much fuller than you think. There were not only the living around you but also the dead were in the church of Halmar, I and many others. We shall now be able to cross the threshold to another world because it has become light and we can see the way."

Then it seemed to Harald Haller as though he had celebrated divine service today for the first time in his life.

It was on the same Sunday that Aaron Mendel strode through the streets of Halmar. He walked upright as never before, and he carried his heavy pack on his back as though it were a toy. The people were surprised, but he told them that now he wouldn't be coming back any more. Then he left Halmar and went to the House of Shadows and to Johannes Wanderer.

"I shall not have to go on my pilgrimage any more, Johannes," he said. "A sign has come that it is so intended, and that is very wonderful. A few days ago when I was carrying my pack along the dusty highroad it suddenly felt light, as if someone had lifted it from me. It is not a burden any more now that I bear for the sake of the ruined Temple. God is propitiated, and he does not desire me to do penance for little Rachel any more. I will go home and play with her in the days that remain to me."

"I am glad about that," said Johannes Wanderer, and he thought of Veronica's dream. "It has been in other respects too a strange Sunday, Aaron. There were both living and dead in the church of Halmar to attend the service. For it has become light in the church of Halmar, and we will believe and hope that it is going to become light everywhere, step by step. Then the ruined Temple will be rebuilt."

"Johannes, can you not tell me who took my heavy burden from me?"

"Everyone must find that out for himself, Aaron, but I think it was someone who understood as no other could have done that you bore your burden for love of little Rachel."

"Then it must be a great and good spirit, Johannes."

"That He most certainly is," said Johannes Wanderer.

You who walk the Earth today, think of this and light your candles for the living and for the dead.

CHAPTER VIII

CARNIVAL

HE violins are singing, the flutes are calling an invitation to the dance, and through the distant roll of drums the bells are tinkling —the masked ball of life is about to begin. But when it is carnival time, then winter has come, has it not? The summer of childhood is past, and many a flower in the garden of youth is faded.

So it was too with Little Veronica as she grew older and the carnival of life called her with soft seductive voices to its motley waltz. She was now fourteen years old, and autumn and winter had descended on many a phase of her life where once spring and summer had blossomed. Mutzeputz too had passed over to another world, and that was the darkest day that Little Veronica had ever known. For the first time she had closed a grave in the full consciousness of her soul, and she knew that what this small grave held was the dearest friend of her childhood and with him her childhood itself. Was this now an end, or was it the beginning of something new and unknown? In life something is always ending, Little Veronica, and something else beginning; and yet it never really ends or begins for it is timeless, and the essence of it goes with us through all days and hours, joyful and sad. And when we close a grave we build a bridge with it to the other world. From year to year there are ever more of these bridges, and in the end we ourselves pass over the many bridges we built in tears and forget that we ever wept over them. The tears are the tribute exacted by the spiritual worlds. All knowledge proceeds through pain to the light, and the one great answer that we hope to find demands to be sought with a thousand fearful questions.

It was a fearful question that stirred in Little Veronica as she wove a little wreath for the grave of her playmate.

"Uncle Johannes," she said, "do you believe that Mutzeputz is all right and that I shall see him again? I'm sure animals must live on just as people do."

Johannes Wanderer was quiet and sad. He had been attached to Mutzeputz too, and both people and animals were creatures equally near to him. Only small souls are conceited enough to presume human superiority over animals.

"I certainly believe that all is very well with Mutzeputz, Veronica," said Johannes Wanderer. "He is in the Garden of God like all living things. Only it is mostly rather less conscious and personal with animals than with people. They go back more into a group; but all these are stages, and they are very difficult for human beings to understand. There are also

many people who are not fully conscious and who
live like animals, embedded in the body of a group, a
nation, a tribe, or a family. Only strong souls pull
themselves up out of these compartments toward the
future human race. The path winds slowly upward,
Veronica. A child in its mother's womb is also an Ego,
but it is not yet awakened. But now is a time of
change, and animals are awakening more and more
from the womb of their group and struggling more
into consciousness. That is why it is so very important
that people look on them as their brothers. In this
way we all have to grow together into a world that
is better and happier than the existence of today.
We have to build this world and help to prepare it,
and in it men and animals will all be more conscious
and enlightened."

"But I want to see Mutzeputz again," insisted
Veronica.

"That you certainly will," said Johannes Wanderer. "Listen, not all lions, for instance, are awakened to their personality. They come from their group
and return to it, just as many people are not yet personalities. But people move from one folk soul to another, while lions remain in the mother-thought of
the lion. But when the lion of St. Jerome went over,
he had become so much of a personality in the love
of the saint that he never returned entirely to the
mother-thought of the lion. He remained what he had
been with his saint; he continued to follow him and
is now, in full awareness, creating the true nature of
lions in the Garden of God. That is all difficult and

cumbersome to explain in human words, but it is
something like the lion of St. Jerome with all animals
who have been able to receive and give much love;
they remain with their mother-soul, but are more
conscious in love and light and as helpers for all the
others. So you will meet Mutzeputz again when you
get to the Garden of God. He will be working on his
part and you on yours; your tasks are different, but
what you have been to each other will remain, for
your relationship was one of love, and love is the secret of all life. Everything proceeds by degrees and
by stages, but what love has created is imperishable
and from it everything is formed from the womb to
the Ego. One must sense this and not try to understand it with the intellect, for it belongs to the great
and the infinite, a part of God's thoughts that are rebuilding the ruined Temple."

It was good for Little Veronica to hear this. So
the gloom of her darkest day was not without light,
and gradually, when she thought of Mutzeputz, she
saw a garden of peace and her soul built a bridge to
him. But now the summer of her childhood was past;
she knew that. Now it was winter, with snow and ice.
The fire was burning in the great tiled stove, and it
cast a flickering light through the dusk of the House
of Shadows and over the many thresholds and steps.
The House of Shadows was snowed in. The northern
winter is long and severe, and it is a good thing that
the stars shine so brightly in the sky.

Little Veronica, you have crossed a difficult, dark
threshold, but there are many other thresholds and

steps in the House of Shadows that you will have to cross. Don't fall, Little Veronica, and remember that even over the House of Shadows stand the eternal stars.

Winter has come, but is not winter the time for carnival? The violins are singing, the flutes calling an invitation to the dance, and through the distant roll of drums the bells are tinkling—the masked ball of life is beginning. Has it not begun for you too, Little Veronica? Does it not seem as if people were beginning to look different? They wear unfamiliar clothes, prettier or uglier than before, and they have masks before their faces that they used not to have. Or is it that until this hour you have only seen the masks, and that now people have taken them off and look at you as they really are? It is seldom in life that one knows whether someone is wearing a mask or whether he has laid it aside. And when do you yourself wear the mask and when not? The Carnival of Life is a crazy dance. We laugh and weep, we hope and stray, we hate and love in its motley waltz, but do we really know who we are and who all the others are? There are so many masks; who can find his way among them? It is often very difficult, Little Veronica, and the hour that really shows us all without our masks is our last hour, and then we shall dance no more in the Carnival of Life.

It was winter, and snow had fallen on many things.

But the violins were singing, the flutes calling, and in the distant roll of drums the bells were tinkling. Carnival comes in winter, does it not? So was it not natural that Ulla Uhlberg should give a masked ball at Castle Irreloh?

Veronica was dressed for the party at Irreloh. She stood in front of the looking glass and stretched her limbs as though preparing for a fight. She looked victoriously young in her gay dress, and Master Mützchen was sitting nearby in a cardboard box regarding her benevolently. A fine gold circlet such as the Florentine ladies used to wear was drawn like a shining thread through Veronica's hair. Caroline had placed her entire collection of printed headscarves at Veronica's disposal, but Caroline's scarves were outside any period and any style, and she had been tactfully dissuaded. Peter and Zottel were standing a little apart admiring Veronica. It was certainly all the same to Zottel how she was dressed. Animals like us just as much if we go in royal robes or in rags. But Peter thought Veronica beautiful beyond measure and almost regretted that he too was not going to the masked ball at Irreloh. Ulla Uhlberg had invited him, it is true, but he was too shy to venture among so many strangers.

"You are very beautiful, Veronica," he said, absorbed.

Veronica was pleased and fingered her jewelry, a little embarrassed.

Had not Peter changed too since their childhood? Was he also wearing a mask? The violins were singing, the flutes calling; the Carnival of Life had begun.

And did not other people also look different in her eyes than formerly, for instance Uncle Johannes? Veronica considered this. Then she threw her head back.

"I must look nice if I am going to Irreloh," she said.

"The men will be astonished when they see you, Veronica," said Peter.

There was a strange undertone in his voice. Veronica felt it.

"I don't care about the men," she said haughtily.

"Not even me, Veronica?" asked Peter softly.

"Oh, you," said Veronica, laughing. "I don't count you when I speak of the others."

What Veronica said to her playmate was well meant, but Peter felt left out. He knew that he could not belong with the others. He hung his head and his hand gripped Zottel's hair, seeking help as he had always done as a little boy when he needed support. The dog had grown older with Peter, and he understood every emotion in the intimidated soul of the simple boy.

Veronica realized that Peter was hurt.

"You mustn't take it that way, Peter," she said warmly. "You and I are just like we've always been to each other, and it would be much nicer if you were coming too, so you could protect me."

"Uncle Johannes will be there," said Peter.

A delicate color flew into Veronica's face.

"Oh, yes," she said self-consciously, "of course Uncle Johannes will be there."

Master Mützchen peeped out of his cardboard box and grinned. Veronica thought he had been getting a little uppish lately.

"You look like a queen, Veronica," said Peter slowly. It was hard for him to form the words for what he wanted to say. "I'd love to make a poem to you like the knights used to do for their queens. But I can't. I still can't write. I can only print the letters separately but I can't join them together. No, I simply can't; there's something missing. Oh, Veronica, I often feel as if it's night around me. I can't describe it any other way; that's what it's like."

Peter looked very sad.

Veronica gripped his hands and looked straight into his eyes, which slowly filled with tears.

"One day the morning will come, Peter. Believe me."

"I believe you," said Peter reverently.

A few minutes later Veronica drove in a sleigh through the winter evening to Castle Irreloh.

*

Do you know the northern winter night? Do you know what it is like to glide on smooth runners over a carpet of glittering snow? Everything is white far and wide, and where it ends is a bluish dusk studded with golden stars. The branches of the fir trees bend under the weight of the snow, and when you pass lonely farms like a softly flying shadow, a dim light shines from the window and sparkling icicles hang from the snow-clad roofs. Everything is strangely

veiled, as though only half real, and covered with a
mantle of a thousand crystals. But it is the king's
mantle of the fairy tale; it shines with countless diamonds, and underneath the essence of life breathes
hotter than ever in the biting cold. It is as though
nothing were impossible, as though enchanted miracles and blue flowers would blossom out of the ice
and snow—and you glide on and on into the infinite! . . .

This is how Veronica drove to Castle Irreloh.

"Carnival in Florence" Ulla Uhlberg had called
her party, and all the varied costumes in the candle-
lit ballroom were to bring the South to the snowy
night of Irreloh. She had sent for costly flowers from
hothouses; they nodded in cut-glass vases and breathed
the scent of summer into the hearts and senses of the
guests.

But Irreloh was not Florence. Were there not
still faded wreaths from bygone times hanging in the
old passages and halls, invisible and woven by invisible hands? Strangely their musty smell blended
with the breath of the fresh flowers, but no one noticed this. Did not a ghostly firelight flicker through
the festive candles, and did not creeping shadows de-
tach themselves from the gray walls to mix with the
dance of the living? Could no one read the signs and
letters of Irreloh?

Irreloh is not Florence, Ulla Uhlberg. But you
have called forth the spirits of both, and now they
stand around you and are dancing with you. Take
care how you handle them. Will not each want some

part of your soul? Have you not lighted this blaze of candles for them and thrown the fresh flowers to them? The violins are singing, the flutes calling an invitation to the dance, and on the gay costumes the bells are tinkling. But far away the surf is singing its song. Think of this, Ulla Uhlberg. In the midst of the giddy dance is there not a weeping in the violins, a lament in the flutes, and in the bells sounds of broken glass? But who wants to think of that? Today is her party that she has prepared for him, today as once before, perhaps—the Carnival of Florence!

And Veronica danced untiringly, with the whole youthful energy of a first experience, pleased that she was sought after and that people admired her. Often it seemed to her too that it was not the first time that she had danced in such a dress with shining jewels in her hair in a candle-lit ballroom—had it not happened before, a long time ago? Veiled, elusive, a distant memory wakened in her of that night of dreams that began with the dreadful man in the red cap and with the singing of the Marseillaise. Had not one of those pictures she plunged into been Florence, and had not Uncle Johannes and Ulla Uhlberg been there as they were today? Yes, it seemed to her that Ulla had been there, just as she was today and in a similar dress. But the violins sang, the flutes called, and Veronica thought no more of the night of the many pictures. Today she was here in Irreloh; today she was young and gay and happy. Why should she think of anything else? Only fleetingly, for a moment, her thoughts turned to her playmate alone at home. She felt sorry for him, but it was a good thing he had not come. People would have recognized the poor boy under the mask. But the Carnival of Life had laid hold of her, and she yielded with all her senses, and above all when Johannes Wanderer danced with her she felt as though the people, candles, and flowers faded away and time stood still.

Little Veronica, time never stands still—and the clocks of Irreloh struck hour by hour. . . .

Veronica was among the last guests to leave.

She looked in vain for Johannes Wanderer. Perhaps he was in one of the other sleighs; there were so many. The horses started, and the sleigh glided through the winter night. Veronica shivered and wrapped her silk shawl more closely around her neck and shoulders. She felt as though she were feverish.

The snow fell in great flakes.

*

In the ballroom at Irreloh there was that stale, after-the-party atmosphere of burned-out candles and fading flowers. The Carnival of Life is always followed by Ash Wednesday. A forgotten mask lay on the brocaded furniture here and there. How many really took off their masks today; how many kept them before their faces? How foreign to each other are nearly all people who are gathered together for a few fleeting hours by the singing violins and the seductive flutes.

Ulla Uhlberg stood facing Johannes Wanderer. They were alone in the ballroom.

"Johannes," she said, "come up with me for a moment. I want to end this day with you. It was our Carnival, the Carnival of Florence!"

Johannes Wanderer followed her silently.

Ulla Uhlberg's boudoir was furnished in a soft red. It contained old Italian furniture, and its gold mountings shone in the light from the candelabra. Red roses stood in a crystal vase beside a sofa. It was very quiet in the room. Over everything was that stillness of extreme fatigue in which one longs to rest and to be somewhere safe out of harm's way.

"Johannes," said Ulla Uhlberg, "wasn't this really the Carnival of Florence? Wasn't it like this once before, and we two were there as well? Do you know when that was?"

"That was a long time ago, Ulla, it was in the year 1527 in Florence."

Ulla Uhlberg turned away.

"That was when the plague came to Florence, Johannes. What a dreadful thought!"

"You know the history of Florence well, Ulla."

Ulla Uhlberg smiled.

"How should I not? I studied it a lot when I was traveling in Italy."

"You have lived through some of this history too, Ulla."

"Do you mean the plague of Florence, as you mentioned that year?"

"Yes, Ulla, that too."

"But, Johannes, that is all over, and if some was ghastly, much of it was very beautiful and it seems to me that I remember it. Can't we go some of this way together again?"

"It is not good to go back, Ulla. When people find one another from past times they should look forward and build anew."

"Then is it wrong, Johannes, to call back a happy hour?"

"It is certainly not wrong, Ulla; it would be foolish to think that spiritual laws are measured by the narrow yardstick of commonplace people. Between two enlightened souls there can be no question of wrong, but what was important then has perhaps now become unimportant. And if you call back one hour, some uncalled things may come too."

Ulla Uhlberg bowed her head in royal humility, as only inwardly great women can do.

"Today it is very important to me," she said softly. "Kiss me once more as you did then, Johannes."

Then Johannes Wanderer bent and kissed Ulla Uhlberg.

Far away a clock struck. A rose moved in the crystal vase and strewed its petals silently on the floor.

*

Johannes Wanderer went out alone into the cold, clear winter night. It had stopped snowing, and the stars were golden in the sky.

Ulla Uhlberg remained in her boudoir dreaming with parted lips. Her foot touched the rose petals on the carpet.

Then she rose and stretched her limbs triumphantly in front of the long glass. Yes, she was beautiful, today as then; she was the noble Florentine lady from those bygone years—when was it? 1527, Johannes had said. Today had been her carnival, the carnival of her life, the Carnival of Florence!

She wanted once again to look at her own reflection, which had intoxicated Johannes, him whom she had loved then, loved today, and would always love. And even if this were going backward, she could think of no more wonderful path to take! Or was it unimportant, as Johannes thought? Ah, no; it was certainly not that to her.

Ulla Uhlberg laughed happily and looked in the glass.

But it was not her reflection that the glass showed. A gaunt skeleton in rags stood there with a flail in its yellow, bony hands, and with a mask before its face. Now it lowered the mask, and a horrible death's head stared at her from empty sockets. The plague of Florence!

Ulla Uhlberg screamed and fled to her bedroom.

That night was not a night of carnival, and Ulla Uhlberg did not dream of the kisses of her beloved. She saw torches in dark streets, shrouded figures that bore covered biers, and she heard the church bells plaintively toll the Miserere. It was the Carnival of Florence that she had called up.

She awoke early and tried to forget the feverish specters of the night. That was all nonsense and imagination! Only the kisses that she had exchanged with

Johannes were real. And was she not young and beautiful and strong enough to face any ghosts?

She looked out of the window. Perhaps she would be able to see the tracks of Johannes' footsteps in the snow. He had gone through the park to the House of Shadows. But fresh snow had fallen, and everything lay deep under a white covering. How quickly all footprints of a person are gone! Snow falls on them through the night, and it is as though no foot had ever passed this way. . . .

Ulla Uhlberg pulled herself together.

The traces of the beloved might be snowed under—in her they still burned. The hours of yesterday beat in her heart and sang in her blood! Only that was living; everything else was shadows and feverish dreams. No, it was not a path backward; she would not have it that it was a path backward. The dreadful specter in the glass of last night was nothing but delusion; it must be that, and she would prove it to herself. She would not permit any shadows on her sunny path! If there had been anything real in that apparition, the glass must bear some proof of it. She would look for this proof; she would go at once, and the empty glass would reveal nothing but her own proud and beautiful reflection!

Ulla Uhlberg stood before the long glass in her boudoir and looked into it. A wide crack showed along its crystal surface from top to bottom.

The plague of Florence had left its mark.

The day after the Carnival at Irreloh was a quiet, rather gloomy winter's day. Johannes Wanderer sat reading, deep in an old book, alone in the Green Room. This room had become more cheerful and brighter, and the picture book of the Gray Lady no longer led its ghostly half-life there. For the Gray Lady had left the House of Shadows and had long since passed over the threshold into another world. That had happened when it became light in the church of Halmar, and the living and the dead worshiped there together.

Now Veronica came into the Green Room, and Johannes Wanderer lowered his book. Veronica sat down beside him.

"Am I disturbing you, Uncle Johannes?"

"No, Veronica, but why are you looking so solemn?"

Veronica put her head on one side.

"Did you stay very long last night at Irreloh, Uncle Johannes?"

"No, Veronica, not very long. I walked home. It was a fine night. I needed a change after the excitement and flurry of the masked ball. Did you enjoy yourself, child?"

"I think I am not a child any more, Uncle Johannes. Last night I went to a carnival with grown-up people. It was very nice, but I didn't like it when you danced with Ulla Uhlberg."

"Why should I not dance with Ulla Uhlberg?" asked Johannes Wanderer kindly.

Master Mützchen crouched apprehensively under the picture of the Gray Lady.

"Don't fall, Little Veronica," he called softly.

"Don't go over this threshold; it is a thorny path for you."

Veronica only heard Master Mützchen as from a great distance. High behind her stood the Angel with the candlestick and the three candles. The red flame burned wildly and flickered. It was bigger than the other two. But Veronica did not see this. The red light blinds our eyes to the tortuous paths and twists of life when it burns more strongly than the blue and the gold flames.

"Why, Uncle Johannes?" asked Veronica shyly. "Because I would have liked to dance with you myself; because I want to have you all to myself, because I love you, Uncle Johannes, that's why."

Her lips trembled with suppressed tears.

Johannes Wanderer took Veronica carefully and cautiously in his arms, as though she were a piece of very fragile crystal.

"Look, Veronica," he said, "it is beautiful that you love me, and I love you too more than anyone else. But I cannot belong to you alone, child. Those people who secretly wear the silver armor, which you have seen too, are sent forth with a task which they have to fulfill. They may not belong to one person alone, because they have to serve this task. It is often hard for them and for others, but it is a burden that they have taken upon themselves. You must understand that, Veronica."

Veronica nodded.

"I know you love me, Uncle Johannes. But I love you differently. I love you the way Peter loves me."

Johannes Wanderer stroked her hair with an infinitely tender touch.

"We loved each other that way once, Veronica. That was in a former life, in Paris. We will not wish that back. As it is now, it is better for the present time, believe me."

"Don't fall, Little Veronica; there are so many steps in the House of Shadows," whispered Master Mützchen under the picture of the Gray Lady.

"It is like this, Veronica," continued Johannes Wanderer. "The masquerade of life has begun for you, and the red light in your candlestick is flickering. It must calm down and lean toward the gold flame as the blue light did. Then all three will burn in peace together, and yesterday, today, and tomorrow will rest in one source of being. You must learn to come to terms with your soul; otherwise you will take too heavy a burden on your shoulders, more than is intended for you. I know that Peter loves you, but this time it is not possible for you to walk your path at the side of the retarded boy. That too is a skein from times past, and now is not the time to unravel it. And if you love me as Peter loves you, that too is a burden that is too heavy for you. For you see, since the last time we were together and loved each other, I have gone a little way forward. Now I am looking back and waiting for you to catch up with me. But for that you must forge for yourself the silver armor, and that is what you wished too, Veronica, on the day when you saw the fortress of Montsalvat in the sun. That is what God sent you to Earth for this time, and when you succeed, then we shall walk together again as once we did when we loved each other. Today I am only here to help you. I can give you all that I have to give, but I may take no gift from you, Veronica. But we will give ourselves to each other again when you have learned to carry the shield of the Grail."

Veronica looked up at Johannes Wanderer.

"I believe I can understand that," she said slowly, "but how shall I gain the shield and armor, Uncle Johannes?"

"That is a hard path, Veronica; it leads over many thresholds and steps. But you are brave and good, and you have come a good way already. There are many burdens which one must bear patiently, as old Aaron Mendel did. The burden that you spoke of, however, you must not take on yourself. It would be too heavy for you, Little Veronica."

Veronica gazed wide-eyed into the distance.

"I will seek and find the shield and armor, and then we will walk together, absolutely and for always, Uncle Johannes, won't we?"

Then Johannes Wanderer kissed Little Veronica on the forehead, and the picture of the Gray Lady smiled. A ray of sunlight broke through the clouds outside and caught itself in Veronica's hair.

*

That night Veronica saw her Angel standing before her. He held the candlestick with the three candles high over her. The red light flickered and quivered restlessly, like the heartbeat of Little Veronica.

Then the Angel spread his hand over it, and gradually the red flame grew stiller and stiller. It leaned toward the golden light in the middle, and Veronica slept.

That night there was a great peace in the House of Shadows. But it was sharply interrupted, and Veronica awoke suddenly.

The bells of Halmar were sounding the storm signal. A bright light blazed like distant sheet lightning. Master Mützchen clambered onto the window-sill and looked out.

"Castle Irreloh is burning!" he called. "The red demons have stoked up their secret fire under the embers again with the hot candle-flames of Ulla Uhlberg's carnival."

The bells of Halmar wailed and lamented loudly in the cold winter's night. Around Ulla Uhlberg's castle the surf sang its old song of the ghosts seeking their lost wreckage, and from the tower the red demons of Irreloh cast the glare of their burning torches far and wide across the land over the white snow.

CHAPTER IX

MORNING

IDNIGHT is past, and the morning is come."

It was the Master who came to Johannes Wanderer and spoke these words. How he comes and how he goes—who may say? There are mysterious things which come to pass in the circle of the Brothers of the Grail, and they happen there where this world and the other merge. Those who only walk the surface of the Earth know nothing of these things.

It was in the garden-house, and it was night. Johannes Wanderer was sitting at his simple, bare desk, and on it he had lighted three candles which he watched over as an image of the three candles of Little Veronica. For it was her soul he was thinking of when the Master came to his aid.

"It is very dark on Earth," said the Master. "It has never been so dark. But the deepest gloom is past. The hour of the world is striking, and it draws toward morning. But the new day brings conflict with it, so that the Morningland of Mankind may rise again."

"I know that," said Johannes Wanderer. "I am prepared for any hour I may be called."

"Many great events will come to pass in this turning point of the world," said the Master, "so that men may awake and comprehend that the hosts of White and Black are battling for their souls. The Grail needs all its warriors. Veronica too has been called, and it is for her sake that I came."

"Veronica will stand at my side when we are called," said Johannes Wanderer. "But I am afraid for her, and I was longing for you to come and help me. Veronica is pure and ready, but she has wandered off the path. She ought not to carry the burden that she wants to take on herself; it is against her destiny."

In the face of the Master were understanding and goodness, and both were infinitely great.

"It is not a real thing," said he. "It is a relic in her of little Madeleine Michaille, which still has to fall away. Her love at that time came to too abrupt and terrible an end."

"Perhaps it is a piece of youthful folly, which comes today and goes tomorrow," said Johannes Wanderer. "It may be that another soul is destined for her when her red flame flares up again. She is still so very young."

"That is not it," said the Master. "She has not many souls near to her in this world. She has journeyed far, and the skein of her destiny is now disentangled. She will not join herself to any other, and this time she is not destined for a long road on Earth.

Only, she must overcome what still remains with her
of little Madeleine. And her red flame must burn in
some more ethereal substance; then she will be puri-
fied and ready for the Grail. This is necessary, for the
Grail needs all its warriors. But she should not lay
on herself a burden heavier than the one that has still
to be borne. Otherwise she will go astray."

"I would so much like to help her carry this burden," said Johannes Wanderer. "Aaron Mendel, too,
carried his burden cheerfully for little Rachel."

"One cannot carry all the burdens for others,"
said the Master. "It is against the law. But here you
can make many of them lighter, if you wish it."

"I will do anything, if it is good for Veronica,"
said Johannes Wanderer.

"It is this way," said the Master. "We can take
this burden from her and lay it on your shoulders.
But it will be no light weight for you. Do you want
that?"

"Yes," said Johannes Wanderer. "I will do anything for Veronica."

"We will do it," said the Master. "Help her, and
we will help you."

Then the Master left him. How he comes and
how he goes—who may say? There are mysterious
things which come to pass in the circle of the Brothers
of the Grail, and they happen there where this world
and the other merge. One can only relate them in
simple words, for they are very great.

Johannes Wanderer stayed behind alone. It was

a lonely and still night through which he kept vigil, and before him on the bare desk burned the candles as an image of the three candles of Little Veronica.

*

It cannot be said that Little Veronica died. It was different from the way it happens to most people. Life and death are so very varied among souls who travel this Earth.

We come from distant heights, and to a far-off land we make our homeward journey. Yet is all distance near when it is fully comprehended.

It came about that Little Veronica grew tired and gradually fell asleep in this world. But to fall asleep in this world is to awaken in another world. It cannot exactly be said that Veronica was sick; at any rate it was not noticeable in the usual way. Winter disappeared, spring and summer blossomed, and Little Veronica grew ever more and more tired. But she did not suffer with this weariness. Only the others suffered, and there was a great silence at this time in the House of Shadows.

Autumn came, and the leaves fell in the garden.

Then the Angel appeared to Veronica in her room as she lay in bed.

"Morning is come, Veronica," said he.

Veronica rose, hardly feeling as if she had left her body. She had outgrown the garment of the Earth, and it is with grace that the Grail escorts those whom it calls.

Master Mützchen stood nearby with his red hat in his hand, tears running down his cheeks. It is very seldom that these beings weep.

"Must I stay behind alone in the House of Shadows?" he asked.

The Angel gazed at him.

"It is a little early for you, Master Mützchen," he said, "but you wept. Tears are the tribute for the Garden of God. Come with us."

Then Master Mützchen hurried along on his thin legs beside the Angel and Veronica as they left the House of Shadows together. High over them the Angel held the candlestick with the three candles of Little Veronica, and the golden light in the middle cast its pure clear glow across the path into the other world.

In the garden the leaves fell and the flowers were withered. Yet it was again a Garden of Spirits like that which Veronica had once known as a little girl.

The animals lay wrapped in their winter sleep, but they all looked up.

"Blessed be your path, Veronica," they said. "You journey toward Montsalvat; help us to our deliverance."

The Elf in the tree nodded to Veronica, and the Water Sprite of the spring threw her shining bubbles high into the air.

"Snow White is asleep in the glass coffin," she called. "Remember that and help her and all of us to awaken, Little Veronica."

Deep under the earth the seeds of the plants

stirred and spoke of the spring that must come, and among the stones in the dark there blazed a luster as of diamonds.

Now they were standing before the Silver Bridge, and the sylphs with colored butterfly wings hovered around them.

"Now you are like us, Veronica," they said.

Everything was as it had been long ago when Veronica was still a child, and yet it was different; it was larger and deeper in intensity.

There where the bridge began, the earth and the stones were as clear as glass, and around them blossomed lilies and roses filled with light, and a thousand other flowers.

"See how white our blossoms are," said the spirits of the Lilies. "So pure and so white is the heavenly garment you are now wearing again."

"Look how red our cups are," said the Rosesouls. "So pure and so red is the Chalice of the Grail, to which you stretch out your arms again today."

Silently and without weight the figures of human beings and animals glided over the bridge, and they too were filled with the same light that illuminated flowers and stones.

Weightlessly, like them, Veronica trod the Silver Bridge, holding Master Mützchen by the hand lest he should be separated from her.

At the edge of the Bridge stood a black figure. Veronica hesitated a moment.

"Don't be afraid, Veronica," said the Angel reassuringly. "You don't have to look him in the face.

This time you are going guiltless across the Silver
Bridge. He who stands there leads those human souls
who would not see the light down, into the valleys of
the deep, until they learn to find their way up into
the Garden of God. Most souls journey first through
the valleys of the deep, and wearisome are the paths
they must walk. They themselves have willed it, for
men and animals accuse them, and they must atone."

Veronica passed by the black figure. He did not
look at her.

Veronica glanced down into the valleys of the
deep. Very deep they were, and there were many
dark and tortuous paths in them. But all paths lead up
to the summit and to the light.

Now the Silver Bridge ended and passed over
into a crystal sea. It was clear and moved unceasingly,
alive in itself but without waves. Veronica plunged
into it, but she did not go under. This, too, she had
already experienced that night of the many pictures.
But then it had been only a small part; now it stretched
into Eternity. The water was all delicate drops of
pearl, and it penetrated her completely. The weariness
of the last Earth life was lifted from her all at once,
and it seemed to her that her whole being was lib-
erated and renewed, as once before in the morning of
the world.

The Angel reached his hand out to her, and she
climbed out again. Master Mützchen was beside her
and skipped over the water on his thin legs.

Now her vision broadened, and she saw countless islands covered with blossoming gardens.

"You have passed by the black figure and over the valleys of the deep," said the Angel. "There is another who calls you, and I will lead you to Him."

Then Veronica looked up and saw Jesus Christ standing before her. She recognized Him, for He looked the same as the One who had lifted the heavy pack from old Aaron Mendel on the dusty highroad. There went out from Him over all the islands and the Gardens of God in the crystal sea a brightness as of the Morning Star.

He stretched out His hand to Veronica.

"We all rejoice that you are here, Veronica," said He with a simplicity and goodness that was greater and more godlike than the whole world of miracles around Him. "Your garden is waiting for you. Tend it further."

Veronica could not bring out a single word. But a feeling of homecoming came over her such as she had never known.

An island floated over the sea to her and came to rest in front of her.

"This is your garden, Veronica," said the Angel.

Veronica stepped ashore over white sand and glistening shells. The treetops rustled gently overhead, and a thousand blossoms opened their cups. Birds sang in the branches, and animals and strange fairy-tale beings flitted all around the garden. But none harmed any other; all these were at peace with one another, for it was the Garden of God and the Morningland of creation.

And there in the midst of it, among blossoming

flowers, sat Mutzeputz, glowing from within and flooded round about with light.

Then Veronica dropped to her knees and cried. It was an inner weeping of the soul, without tears and without pain, like the trembling of a chord stretched to the breaking point.

Veronica's island glided out into the crystal sea past other floating islands. Everywhere familiar faces looked over and greeted her—spirits from many former lives whom she saw again. It was so much all at once, and a strange, blissful longing for sleep stirred in her, the fulfillment of peace and freedom from desire.

"We will come and visit you soon," called the spirits from the other shores. "We are so delighted that you are here again. You have been away a long time, and we have longed for you."

"Now rest, Veronica," said the Angel. "When you wake again, tend your garden. And now, look out there over the sea. There lies Montsalvat, its gates and towers shining in the morning light. Your island is floating toward its shores. There you will learn to forge the shield, the sword, and the silver armor, for the Grail has summoned you."

Then Veronica lay down among the blossoming flowers in her garden, Mutzeputz and Master Mützchen in her arms. And there she slept, a child safe from harm, and knew in full consciousness her childhood and her salvation. Conscious childhood is blessedness.

The Angel placed the candlestick on an altar at

their heads, and in the pure golden flame burned the three candles of Little Veronica in the Garden of God.

Meanwhile the island floated slowly in the morning light across the crystal sea toward the shores of Montsalvat.

*

It was a dark and heavy day in the House of Shadows as the earthly body of Little Veronica was laid to rest.

"More has turned to ashes for all of you than for me, Johannes," said Ulla Uhlberg. "But we will build again; that is our destiny."

"I will try," said Johannes Wanderer.

Peter spoke never a word. He buried his face helplessly in Zottel's hair.

Aaron Mendel was there too. He did not walk upright, as he had done when last seen, but was bowed as before when he still carried his heavy pack. He knew that the burden which those in the House of Shadows bore today was heavier than all the burdens he had ever carried.

The rain streamed down. In the garden the leaves fell.

*

It was a severe winter, and the House of Shadows was snowed in. But even the deepest winter goes over and the spring comes. The ice, cracking and bursting, had rushed down the rivers into the wild sea breakers. The first green veil hung on the birch trees, and the anemones bloomed in the wood.

Johannes Wanderer stood in the garden digging the earth for a new planting. Crocuses and violets were already out. Life was beginning once more. But Johannes Wanderer had aged. The burden of this winter had been too heavy, and he still carried it.

Now he looked up from his work. Peter was hurrying through the garden gate and came running up to him with Zottel. This was not his way as a rule; he was quiet and slow in everything. The boy's face shone with a strange inner joy, and the perplexed, inquiring eyes had cleared a little.

"I dreamed about Veronica last night, Uncle Johannes," he cried. "She looked so wonderful, all white and bright, and she said to me: 'Morning is come. Peter, go to Uncle Johannes and tell him this.' "

Johannes Wanderer lowered his spade.

" 'Morning is come'?" he repeated slowly. "Did she say that?"

"Yes, Uncle Johannes, and Ulla Uhlberg is coming here too. She's just arrived and I've told her already. Veronica told me too that I should write down what she had said to me. I'm going to do it."

"Can you write now, then, Peter?"

"I believe so," said the boy.

Johannes Wanderer went into the house and brought Peter paper and pencil.

"If you believe it, then you can do it. Try to write it down."

Peter sat down and laid the paper carefully on his knee. Then he wrote in large clumsy letters, but all connected: "Morning is come."

There were tears in his eyes. Johannes Wanderer and Zottel stood nearby as witnesses of Peter's first handwriting.

This was a great moment in the life of the simple boy and those who cared for him.

Along the path came Ulla Uhlberg.

"Peter can write," Johannes Wanderer said to her. "He has written that morning is come. Veronica told him this."

"Then let it be morning for all of us, Johannes. Look. I too have learned to accept my life, and in it to accept and sanctify all life. I will build Irreloh up again; but differently from the way it was. It shall be a help to human beings and animals; there are so many who need help. For you and Peter too there will be much to do. If I accept life this way, Johannes, will you help me with it?"

"Yes, I'll do that, Ulla," said Johannes Wanderer.

"Together we will dig the earth for a new planting, for the Morningland of the living and the dead."

And he dug his spade deep into the moist spring earth.

*

That night Johannes Wanderer sat up a long time, and again before him burned the three candles as an image of the three candles of Little Veronica. It was quiet and peaceful, but very, very lonely in the garden-house.

It was toward midnight when it grew light in the

room, and Veronica stood there. She looked taller
than before, like a fully grown young girl.

"Johannes," she said softly.

"Is it you at last, Veronica?"

"Yes, Johannes. Morning is come."

"The night was dark and long, Veronica."

"I know, Johannes. You took a burden on your
shoulders for me, and I thank you for it. I know too
how heavy a burden it was."

"The burden was heavy because I loved you
very much, Veronica, and because I longed for you
so much."

"I had to rest, Johannes; one lives through so
much on the path the other side of the Silver Bridge.
That is why I didn't come sooner. But I will come to
you often now. I visited Peter too, and I was in the
House of Shadows with Mama and Aunt Mariechen,
but they didn't see me. You must help them to see me,
Johannes."

"I have often tried to, Veronica; I have tried
many times. They are so very deeply imprisoned in
this world. But they are bearing a heavy burden because of you, and they will learn under the load to see
with the eyes of the depths. Be with them often, Veronica; one day they will see you or will sense your
presence. Then they will find peace and the road to
the light."

"I will do it, Johannes, and I will come very often
to you too now. Midnight is past, and the morning is
come. The Grail calls on all its warriors for the Morningland of Mankind. I am forging my silver armor,

shield, and sword, and I will stand at your side when the struggle with the dark powers begins and you hold your shield over the defenseless."

"That is a beautiful thought, Veronica. That is what I have always wished for myself, that you should stand at my side. The prize is worth the battle, and we shall conquer, Veronica."

"Yes, Johannes, we shall conquer, and the ruined Temple will be built up again. Good-bye, Johannes, I'll come again soon."

"Yes, come soon again, Veronica."

Veronica disappeared into the light from which she came.

Johannes Wanderer sat motionless before the candles until they were burned out.

The night was ended. It grew light, and Johannes Wanderer stepped out into the garden.

The sun had risen.

In the young earth of springtime glowed the year's first blossoms in the same morning gold as above in the Garden of God glowed the three candles of Little Veronica.

*

We come from distant heights, and to a far-off land we make our homeward journey. Yet is all distance near when it is fully comprehended.

Build your temples, all you who walk the Earth today, build your mansions, fill them with light. And remember: Midnight is past and the morning is come.

About the Author

MANFRED KYBER was born in 1880 in Riga, Latvia, on the Baltic coast that later became the setting for his greatest novel. He was the younger of two boys in an old and prosperous Hanseatic merchant family, and his father's country estate offered him a boyhood surrounded by woods, flowers, and animals that he learned to love.

Kyber attended a gymnasium in St. Petersburg and later the University of Leipzig. His decision to be a writer came at the age of 18, and he left school, against his father's wishes, to do so.

From Kyber's pen came poems, fairy tales, and animal stories. He made friends with musicians, poets, and writers such as Selma Lagerlöf. But the sensitive, mystical side of his nature was especially influenced by his meeting in 1911 with Rudolf Steiner, the Austrian philosopher and spiritual scientist, to whom he later dedicated his best known collection of thirty-three poems, *Genius Astri*.

Two collections of Kyber's animal stories *(Unter Tieren*, 1912, and *Neue Tiergeschichten*, 1926) had sold 100,000 copies by 1927 and continue to sell today. An English translation of these, *Among Animals*, appeared in 1967. Collections of his fairy tales *(Märchen)* were republished in 1966. The novel, *The Three Candles of Little Veronica*, written in 1929, has become a household classic in Germany.

Kyber married Elisabeth Boltho von Hohenbach,

also of an old Baltic family, in 1909. Their life was not without suffering. During World War I the Kybers were 'civil' prisoners of the Russians, and when they returned to Germany they were close to starvation.

Kyber's final years were spent in Löwenstein, Germany, where he lived quietly, almost ascetically, in surroundings of austere simplicity. Two years before he died in 1933, he wrote *Neues Menschentum* (A New Humanity) setting forth the ideals he longed to see realized on earth. "Man has two natures, the worldly and the other-worldly," he wrote, "and we can and shall be able to solve the problems of mankind only when we find the synthesis of both in a spiritualized way of thinking."